BONNIE ENGSTROM

Melanie's Blue Skirt

The Candy Cane Girls, book 6

By Bonnie Engstrom

Published by Forget Me Not Romances, a division of Winged Publications

ISBN-13: 978-1-946939-43-2
ISBN-10: 1-946939-43-9

Special Thanks To

Emily and Shane Sullivan and their staff at Spine Scottsdale Physical Therapy. They are all gracious and knowledgeable about, you guessed it – the spine. Actually, all bones in the body, as well as muscles. They know just what to do to take the pain away.

Honor Health Hospital, Scottsdale for, even though I never formally asked, giving me the perfect setting for a unique wedding. For my husband Dave who is on the staff and asked some of the nurses the day we were visiting. How could they turn him down with his wonderful smile?

Pastor George and the Hillsong Church, Scottsdale praise band who inspired me, as they do every Sunday, to have them play at the wedding.

Jaeda Wayman, banker extraordinaire, who was introduced in *Connie's Silver Shoes* and will forever be a huge hero in my Candy Cane Girls Series. This wonderful man is a real banker who was my own personal banker until he was deservedly promoted. He has moved on in his professional life but will continue with his permission throughout the *Candy Cane Girls Series*. He really does like to wear a red business shirt, and he really does have a collection of over 250 basketball shoes. But, everything else about him, except his exceptional character, is fictional. I may feature his photo in a future Life On The Lake newsletter, so sign up on my website www.bonnieengstrom.com to meet him.

A Very Special Note about Lola the dog

As you probably guessed, Lola is a real dog, part of our family, as Jake was in *Connie's Silver Shoes*. I wanted so much for her to be part of the cover of *Melanie's Blue Skirt*, but she did not want to cooperate for a photo op. She is cuddly, but shy. Hubby and I took so many photos, we can't even remember how many, to send to my publisher. Finally, our twelve-year-old granddaughter, Taylor, who is a photo guru stepped in. It's amazing how much young people have mastered technical stuff. Taylor believed she could do it – take a photo of Lola and block out the background so Cynthia, my publisher, could use it on the cover. Taylor worked on it for hours. But, she did it!!

Kudos to Taylor, and thank you to Cynthia for her patience. Great cover!

Dear Reader ~

I hope you will enjoy this series that tells the stories of women who are what I call super friends ~ friends who committed as teenagers to prayer and loyalty bound by a moniker. The Candy Cane Girls are a unique group of sister friends. I hope their stories will inspire other young women. They are Sisters of Promise, promises they made when young and promises they've kept for generations.

I am hoping to start an inspiration, a situation or a way to encourage young women, especially teen girls, to write their own stories. I have three teenage granddaughters who are bright and talented but as far as I know do not record their thoughts and experiences. I also pray for other teen girls of friends. It troubles me they are not writing about their lives and experiences. Please join me in praying for an upcoming of young women writers.

As you read through this series, and I hope you will, please note how each book tells a story about individual women, how each struggle with a personal situation and overcomes it. Some of the circumstances they encounter are destined by faith and fate; but all require belief and commitment to each other and to the faith of each. I hope you will read every story to see how Cindy deals with her new love's health issues, and Candy takes her fears into action, and Connie . . . well she has a problem that she overcomes with the help of sweet Jake, her 'problems solving' dog. Jake will appear in many following books. He was my running companion for many years – the dearest dog. But Lola and Happy Arthur are shining woofers in their own stories.

But wait until you get to Natalie and Melanie! They hold the keys to lasting friendship. Their stories are almost legendary.

All stories in the series can be read individually, but you will enjoy them more and understand them more if you read them in order.

Noelle, Cindy, Connie, Candy, Natalie, Doreen and especially Melanie will steal your heart.
You will have fun with the different wedding venues. How many weddings have you attended in an historical place, or in a hospital lobby or a gym? Maybe these will be your first and most memorable.

You will do me a great favor if you enjoyed this series and write a quick, honest review on Amazon or Goodreads. Just a few words mean a lot and encourage others to read it.

Thank you. If you would like to be connected to me for comments and conversation please sign up for my newsletter at www.bonnieengstrom.com and learn about my writing history. You can email me at bengstrom@hotmail.com. Please put SERIES <in caps) in the subject line. I would love to chat with you.

Special BONUS! The Candy Cane Series is ideal

for group discussion, especially for book clubs. I have a special offer for book clubs for all of my books. If you are interested please email me at bengstrom@hotmail.com with CLUB <all caps) in the subject line.

Blessings,
Bonnie

PROLOGUE
My name is Melanie.

I am the honorary and seventh Candy Cane. As in all the Candy Cane stories, each girl in the sisterhood appears, at least briefly. We are a unique, integral group of friends who pray for each other and whose life situations intertwine. It would be impossible to tell any one of our stories without including the others. So, this story begins with me, and although it does end with me, it includes all seven of us. It also includes some of our family members ~ mothers and fathers and siblings and husbands, even children ~ because they are important parts of our lives.

If you have not read any of the other Candy Cane stories, I hope the brief explanations of each of them gives you some sense of their personal stories. Or, it might be fun to start at the beginning with *Noelle's Christmas Wedding*, then *Cindy's Perfect Dance* and proceed to Candy's frustration and indecision in *Candy's Wild Ride*. Will Candy marry the same man twice? Or, will she give up on him? How about Connie? Can her family accept the handsome banker of another race? Does love cross ethnic and racial lines? Little Jake, the Miniature Pincher doggie, doesn't see a problem in *Connie's Silver Shoes*. But, Natalie, aw . . . Will true love ever come to her? When she is left hurting and abandoned after her sky diving accident, how can she ever trust again? *Natalie's Deception* will bring you to this story.

Did I forget Doreen? Never. Her story begins tragically in *Noelle's Christmas Wedding*. So, how did she become an international sensation? Maybe her story will finally be told in the future.

The fun part is that the Candy Canes go on and on. Little Robby has to grow up sometime, doesn't he? Natalie and I will hopefully find true love . . . sometime. Babies will be born, old boyfriends will return, love and lives will be restored. Enjoy!

Chapter One
Melanie
Searching for Love

"Adopt."

Melanie Carson slammed the door of the small office in Nat's Gym behind her and pulled up the lone uncomfortable visitor chair. Propping her elbows on the desk across from Natalie, she said, "You heard me. I want to be adopted."

Natalie pushed the drugstore glasses down her nose and peered over the wire rims.

"What," Nat asked as she feared the answer, "are you talking about?" She pulled a tissue from the ever-present box on her desk and crumpled it. The wad formed a ball in her hand. She kneaded it tightly like one of those yeast rolls her mom used to make for Thanksgiving dinner. Clearing her throat as quietly as she could, she glanced outside the office door toward the pebbled glass insert. Assured no gym client was hovering there, she focused on her friend, then asked the next question.

"You wanna explain?" Natalie knew Melanie was still recuperating, was that the right word she wondered, from her terrifying experience being stalked by a horrible man, her stepfather. Melanie and her mother Susan shared the same pain about Bruce Walker. The two women were very close, a relationship Natalie envied. She pulled the useless glasses off her nose and plunked them on the never-ending pile of papers on her desk. Why she had papers when everything was online she didn't know. She guessed she was old-fashioned, even at almost thirty. She shoved the pile aside.

Melanie fidgeted, tapped her manicured blue nails on the desktop. "Maybe I didn't say that right."

"I hope not," Nat replied. "Why, at almost thirty do you want to be adopted? Trouble with your mom?" Nat squeezed the ball of tissue harder. What was wrong with Mel?

"I guess I'm nervous about it. I am lonely. I want companionship. I don't want to *be* adopted. I want *to* adopt."

Natalie, always considered the practical one of the Candy Cane sisterhood, pushed her bangs aside and rubbed her forehead. She was confused. Melanie had been accepted into the former high school friendship group several years ago after causing Doreen's accident, then getting the injured woman's forgiveness. She'd envied the close friendship of the Candy Cane swim group and practically begged to be part of them. They initiated her by having her swim ten laps, and she became a stalwart prayer partner. Now, Natalie was worried about Mel's mental health – seeking adoption, or even to adopt, single, and at almost thirty years old?

"Explain." It was a command, not a request.

"Oh. I guess I didn't explain properly?"

"You think?"

Melanie wiggled further into the seat of the uncomfortable chair in the tiny office at Nat's Gym. She had occupied it many times before, but this time was different, although the office was still stuffy for lack of adequate air conditioning. This time she looked like she hoped Natalie would understand and support her. Nat kept peering at her, locking her blue eyes with Mel's brown ones. Both blinked.

Melanie adjusted her skirt, the chambray one she seldom wore. She fiddled with the blue flower pattern making sure it was over her left knee. Blue was her God color, her favorite. Surely Natalie remembered.

She finally got her breath. Why was this such a big deal? God must have led her to this crazy decision. It could mean giving up her independence, her daily routine. She gulped and finally let it out. "I want to adopt a dog."

~

Natalie let out a huge breath that blew a few errant papers from her desk to the floor. "That, is it?" She felt relieved, but still concerned. Melanie was usually very rational and explained things in detail. Like when she explained how she discovered Bryce was the mysterious sky dive instructor who had left Natalie injured on the ground during her solo dive.

The man who had been the sole fitness trainer at Nat's Gym, the man who'd followed Natalie to Scottsdale when she visited Connie and Jaeda, the man who had disappeared prompting Natalie to hire Larry, a private investigator, to find him. As angry as Natalie was at Bryce, she still worried about him. She glanced at the time on her new Fitbit. "If I don't rush, I will be late.

"Can we talk about this later? I have a meeting with Larry the PI who was following Bryce."

"Oh, sure. Guess it's not all that important." Melanie shoved the chair back almost tipping it over so it teetered on the back legs, picked up her purse and sweater, and stormed out the door slamming it. The pebbled glass window rattled a little. Not a lot, but enough so Natalie jotted a note on a sticky pad to have it checked. In the past Bryce would have done that. But, Bryce was no longer part of the gym. The loud engine of Mel's ancient car revved outside.

Natalie lifted her eyes to the ceiling. What was wrong with that girl? Was she really that lonely?

Chapter Two
Natalie
Dream Man? Maybe.

Natalie set her paper cup down and wiggled into the metal chair at the Corona del Mar Starbucks on Pacific Coast Highway. Really, she thought, we should all either pay rent here or have this local patisserie give us free coffee. So many Candy Cane sisters had graced the chairs; some finding love, others cementing friendships. Was it her turn now? She hoped.

The door chimed letting tepid May air in, a preview to a balmy southern California summer. A tall, dark, handsome man entered and looked around. Larry? She had seen his photo on Facetime and was sure it was him, but she held back not wanting to look too anxious. He tugged off large sunglasses and hung them in the neck of his blue starched shirt, pushed his baseball cap back on his head and waved.

To her, or to the patrons in general?

Suddenly the background chatter of other customers stopped. She looked around and noticed couples, even two middle-aged women, were whispering. Eyes seemed to focus in Larry's direction. A few patrons shrugged and got back to sipping coffee. Some were looking at her now. Some back and forth between her and Larry. Then, it hit her. They were looking at his skin color. This is Newport Beach, lily white Newport Beach. Her heart sank for a moment.

Pulling out the chair opposite, he grinned and held out his hand. "You must be Natalie. I recognized your eyes from our Facetime chats." She started to nod, then stood up tall, smiled, and reached for his hand gripping it firmly with both of hers. She hoped she had gotten the message across to the others. He certainly was a handsome guy.

Natalie had let her hair down from its usual ponytail, and loose strands of tawny amber cascaded over her shoulders. She fingered a few on her shoulder, then flipped them back. Was she too obvious? She had been anxious to meet this man who had tracked the errant Bryce through three states. Connie and Jaeda had confidence in his ability, and he had sent text updates all along. She remembered all the text and Facetime updates, but she was curious about the real man. He was just as handsome as the pictures had shown, and his texts were kind and encouraging. Was he the one?

Would he be marriage material?

~

Larry shifted on his feet suddenly aware of the

uncomfortable atmosphere in the coffee shop. Hoping to diffuse the whispers and the quiet stares, he scanned the other patrons and grinned. He tilted his head for a better look at Natalie. Girl was cute, not gorgeous, but cute. She had what he called a winning smile and sparkling blue eyes – like some kind of jewel his mother used to wear. Her eyes were laced with long russet lashes that fluttered when she smiled. Yep, cute girl. Ignoring the customers around them, he smiled directly at her, then tugged again on the opposite chair but didn't sit down. She had clasped his hands and he was rewarded with firmness, a touch he liked. This was no wimpy woman.

"Mind if I grab a Frappuccino?"

Natalie nodded and gestured with her chin toward the counter. She was blushing and smiling, showing her even white teeth. "Can I get you a refill?" Least he could do for this cute girl who had put so much trust in him. Not to mention his hourly PI fees.

"Thanks. I'd like that." Another smile. He heard some veiled whispers from other customers. He still sensed tension in the room. Why were her eyes shifting left and right? Did she know something about him? Could she possibly know? Nah, he felt meeting her was safe.

He put the two paper cups with brown sleeves on the table. She thanked him and fiddled with hers, turning it around several times. If she didn't take a sip soon, all that wonderful foam would disappear. "You're gonna miss the foam if you don't drink it soon. Or, maybe you don't like foam. Not a foam person?" he asked. He was sure his eyes were an invitation.

She giggled and shifted in her chair. He liked her giggle, too. It wasn't childish, but melodic, kind of grown up, and sort of throaty. What was wrong with the Bryce guy he'd been tailing for weeks? Leaving a girl like this? Maybe, if she decided to hire him for more, he would find out, assuming he would be available. Must be something wrong with the guy. Or, maybe he, Larry, hadn't yet found a flaw in Natalie.

Finally, lifting the lid off her cup, she said, "See, I took a sip. Love the foam. Best part." She smiled at him again. "Nice to finally meet you, Larry, but now down to business."

~

Natalie kicked off her shoes and wiggled into the deep softness of her sofa. Meeting Larry had been quite an experience. She liked him a lot and trusted him. He had done a great job following Bryce from California to Arizona to Nevada and back again. Bryce must have sensed he was being pursued, always taking off one step ahead. Was he really that smart? Or, was it just coincidence? Larry had never caught up enough with Bryce to plant a GPS on Bryce's Harley. Yet, she wondered if he was supposed to be such a great PI, why hadn't he? Maybe she was being too suspicious. Where was her trust?

The Larry guy was charming; great smile and glistening charcoal eyes. When he smiled his whole face grinned. She knew he was the most popular guard at the entry gate in the community in Scottsdale where Jaeda and Connie now lived.

Probably because of his courtesy and his friendly personality. Maybe his winning smile.

Big problem, though. He was black. She thought of all the hurdles Connie and Jaeda had leaped over because of their different races. Could she do that? What if Larry wasn't interested, maybe just being polite? What about her family, her friends, her colleagues and patrons at Nat's Gym? She knew she was jumping ahead, way ahead. Time to make a cup of herbal tea and give her concerns up to the Lord. Maybe Melanie had a good idea adopting a dog.

She could have kept the adorable cat, Star, that Cindy foisted on her after Emily had given it to Cindy as a guilt gift for finally accepting that Rob Lovejoy loved Cindy, but didn't love Emily. So confusing. Emily eventually admitted Rob was truly just a supportive AA friend. What a complicated mess, and poor little kitty Star was in the midst. Cindy couldn't take Star to Costa Rica on Rob's and her mission trip, so she donated him back to Emily who burst into Nat's gym office one day and plopped a carrier on her desk. Star popped out and snuggled her. Which was okay until Rob's mom, Lydia Lovejoy, claimed him to be the Love In Bloom Floral store cat sniffing roses all day long. He was gone, a done deal. Hopefully, exploring all the flowery scents with his pink nose at Love In Bloom.

Feeling guilty, but not sure why, she made the call to Melanie.

"You serious about adopting a dog?" She held her breath waiting for Mel's answer.

"I am" she replied. "Went to PetSmart and Petco today. Both have adoptions. Even looked at the cats."

"Cats don't require as much work," Natalie offered. What did she really know?

"Yeh, but they can't run with you," Mel snapped. "You know I run every morning, sometimes in the evening. My routine."

"Did you find one you fell in love with? Pit bulls are supposed to be super lovable and loyal."

"I might have. Gotta go back next weekend and see if the one I felt drawn to is still there."

"What's it like?"

"Weird looking dog, but super cute in its own way. I worry it will never be adopted."

"Aw. Maybe the one for you who can give it a lot of love. Tell me about it."

Chapter Three
Natalie
Loneliness

Natalie's phone chimed, and she rummaged for it. In her purse, again! She had always thought of herself as organized. The Candy Canes did, too. Even dubbed her as "The Organized One" of the group. She had a routine that she tried not to deviate from. Cell phone by the coffee pot was part of it. That side pocket in her purse was, too. She dug deep, shifting makeup and hairbrush and wallet around, as well as change purse and eyeglass case. Where was the errant thing? It kept playing Blue Moon which always reminded her she was still standing alone. Time to change the tune. Finally, she found it and pushed the green button to accept Melanie's call.

"Gosh, girl, took you a long time to answer."

"Sorry. Couldn't find the dratted thing. What's up?"

"I am so excited! I adopted today. Wanna come meet her?"

"Sure. I have to close up the gym, then on my way. What's her name?"

"Lola. Her foster parents gave all nine pups Disney names. Hers was Ariel. Dumb name for a dog. She was number eight in the litter. Couldn't figure that one out. Since today is May 5, Cinco de Mayo Day, I picked Lola. Still Spanish, and she seems to like it."

"Much easier than Ariel for sure. I am on my way." Natalie deliberately put her phone in the pocket of her purse. Should she stop at the market and buy a doggie treat? Or flowers for Mel? Instead, after locking up the gym, she jumped in her little car and headed out.

Nat stopped cold. This was one of the strangest dogs she had ever seen, even on You Tube. She was so ugly she was cute, sort of. The long, low dog wiggled up to her. She petted the tuft of hair on her head, a Mohawk? On a dog? A female dog? The batch of straggly hairs stood upright, very pronounced, kind of bizarre, as were the protruding bushy eyebrows – tenting above very dark orbs. The dog blinked, and Natalie glibly thought *too much eye makeup*. The long, velvet upright ears were the defining characteristic. They stood straight up, always on alert. Natalie thought they and her long muzzle made her look a bit like a deer, or maybe a fox.

"She's so loving," Melanie said. Were there tears in her eyes? "Pick her up. She loves to be cuddled."

Natalie scooped the funny dog into her arms and

sat on the sofa. Lola pushed her long snout under Natalie's arm, then raised her head and insisted on kissing Nat. On the chin. Ugh.

Natalie was not a dog person, not even a pet person. Fish, like Shrimp her Beta were fine. She cleaned his bowl twice a week, fed him (or maybe he was an 'it'), and tapped on the glass when he swam near it. For Melanie's sake, maybe she could get used to this. For a dog, Lola was cute.

~

Nat propped her bare feet on her coffee table. She cradled a Starbucks latte. It left a bitter taste in her mouth. Maybe she should have ordered a Frappuccino. Maybe she should think about adopting a dog. Maybe Melanie was right. Having a companion filled the empty places.

She thought about all the times she was lonely and envied her Candy Cane sisters who had husbands to fill the void. Some also had goals, like Cindy and Rob in Costa Rica still working God's plan to plant a church. Connie had her own design firm, and Doreen modeled for it. Candy, and Mel the dog adopter as she now called her in jest, were preschool teachers as Cindy had been. Noelle was in a league of her own being the most educated with a master's degree in education, teaching senior high school English, Shakespeare of all subjects. Recently, she announced she was pregnant. Nat giggled to herself. Would Braydon and Noelle name the baby Bard if it was a boy?

Was she, Natalie, so undesirable? She dreamed of having a family with a husband who adored her. Maybe her dreams were too high; maybe they weren't God's dreams for her. How would she know? Maybe God had other plans for her. To be alone. She didn't believe that, couldn't believe it. After all, two men, Billy and Bryce, had followed her to Arizona when she visited Jaeda and Connie. As much as she liked them both, they were both fine men (well, maybe Bryce was iffy), but neither made her heart sing. She pulled off her shoes and draped a cotton nightie over her head. Turning off her phone and setting it on the stand next to her bed, she collapsed and snuggled under the fluffy covers. Tonight, she promised herself, she would not dream.

Chapter Four
Melanie
Trouble at Work

Melanie stood stunned in her preschool classroom. Her co-teacher, Nora, had walked out. No goodbye, no explanation. Just left. What had happened? Little Jackson still played with the puddle on the table left over from snack. She was alone, except for the adorable little boy rubbing his finger in the puddle of apple juice and licking it. He looked up to her and his grin almost melted her heart. "Miss Mellie, Mommy not here yet?" he asked innocently. She saw the worry on his small face and rushed to sit beside him on a chair so tiny it almost didn't hold her petite frame.

"Not yet, sweetie. Maybe she got caught in traffic." He grinned again. Apparently, he was okay. His mommy was always late.

She couldn't leave Jackson alone until a parent

picked him up. Was Nora angry? What had made her leave before the expected time? And with a sneer on her face. Searching her brain, she wondered if she had done something wrong to offend her; but still, a professional wouldn't just leave with no explanation.

Jackson's mom, Olivia, finally picked him up fifteen minutes late with profuse apologies. Melanie waved the explanation off reminding the mom to call ahead and explain. Then she went into the office to see the director, hoping Ms. Dana would have some insight and explanation.

Dana waved her in and gestured to a seat. It was late and most teachers and staff had left for the day, still Melanie felt compelled to discuss the Nora situation with her.

Dana nodded her head and her long brown hair skimmed her shoulders. Melanie thought how beautiful she is. Why hadn't some tall, handsome, Christian man scooped her up? Maybe it's the single mother of four children thing. Still, she hoped for Ms. Dana.

"It's frustrating to me, too," Dana said. "I believe whether it's in the contract or not, and it is, it is unprofessional to leave because a teacher doesn't relate to a student. Especially, a three or four-year-old child." She paused and ran a hand across her forehead pushing aside her bangs. Looking at Melanie, she asked, "Did Nora say anything to you? Or, to the child?"

"No, she just stormed out. Well, yes, she did, sort of. When I asked her why she was leaving so abruptly, she said, 'Can't handle this child.' That was all." Melanie took a deep breath and swiped at her eyes with a tissue Dana pressed into her hand.

"She didn't go into detail?"

"No."

"What could little Jackson have done to upset Nora so much?"

"Well, he wiggles in his chair a lot and blows bubbles with his lunch. Sometimes the bubbles spray on other students. Other kids do that, too. He has trouble sitting still, but Johnny and Mary do, too." Melanie paused and leaned forward in her chair. "I worry about Nora," she said. "Maybe teaching preschoolers is not her strength. One does have to have a thick skin and a lot of love." She leaned back in her chair and waited. Maybe she had said too much. She loved Nora her co-teacher, but Nora seemed more sensitive than her.

"I hope I didn't overstep my bounds." Melanie twisted her fingers together.

Director Dana grinned at her. "Not at all. I am glad you gave me an honest report about the Jackson situation." She rose from her chair and clasped Melanie's hands in hers. "It is a problem, and it may continue to be one." She paused and looked up as if asking for Divine wisdom. Squeezing Melanie's hands, she said, "I know the situation, but unfortunately I can't share, it's confidential. I can tell you there is a reason for Jackson's behavior. It is a valid reason." She released Melanie's hands with a squeeze. "I hope you understand."

Melanie nodded through tears and the two women hugged. It was going to be all right, eventually. At least she had Dana's support, and she hoped Dana would confer with Nora.

Back home after a run, Melanie unhooked Lola's leash and tossed her a treat. The dog wiggled and whined. Maybe actually grinned. Melanie laughed.

"You are so cute, Lola." Melanie couldn't resist. Lola was saving her from loneliness. She sipped her homemade latte and snuggled on the sofa. Lola followed, jumping up on her lap and licking her chin. What could anyone want other than this?

Chapter Five
Connie and Jaeda
Problems and Lessons

Connie tugged at the bedding and yanked the down comforter up under her chin. Jaeda reached under the covers for her hand. It was icy cold. "You all right?"

"Just freezing. Guess it's pregnancy hormones. It does seem unusually cold for Arizona." She returned his hand squeeze and he placed a palm on her cheek and turned her head toward him, her chestnut hair cascading across her pale cheek. "You promised me warm, even hot, in Arizona." She trembled. "Sorry. Baby doesn't like it either – lots of kicking going on."

Jaeda shimmied closer to her and wrapped his body around hers. She shook in his arms like a mini earthquake, one he had experienced in California. *Please God, may she be okay, may there be nothing wrong.* He fell asleep with Connie's small frame trembling and her belly filled with their baby vibrating against him.

The next day, during his lunch hour, he called Cindy and Rob in Costa Rica on their special California telephone number. What he got startled him. "Welcome to Coastline Church. Please leave a message and . . ." Rob's voice cut off the answering device with "Hey, Jaeda! How are you? What's up?"

Jaeda almost forgot his reason for calling. "Wow, Rob, a church? You and Cindy actually started one?"

"Well, almost." He heard the sigh on the other end. "Sort of." Jaeda was bothered by the pause. It didn't sound very positive. "We don't have a church building yet, and we only have a few people who attend." his voice picked up, "it's a start. That's not why you called, is it?"

"No. Rob, but please send us information so we can all pray about it." Jaeda took a deep breath. "It's Connie."

"What's wrong? She all right? You sound very concerned."

"I am. I think she's okay, but this pregnancy thing may be getting to her." He stopped to squeeze his nose, an old habit. "She's cold all the time, mostly at night. Last night she was shaking so bad I had to hold her to keep her warm. That was at midnight. Then, she woke me up at four a.m. asking me to go to McD's for a cheeseburger and fries."

Why was Rob laughing? This wasn't funny. He held the phone away from his ear as Rob chuckled.

"Oh, man, you almost got me there." More laughter, more chuckling this time. "Sounds normal to me. At least you have a McDonalds!" More laughter. "We don't have one, not close in Playa Hermosa."

This wasn't what Jaeda had hoped for, or maybe it was. Did he have to go through four more months of this? If it was normal, could he do that? "Rob," he said trying to stifle his impatience, "you serious?"

"Sorry, buddy, yes. But it does get better." He sniggered this time. "Wait until you have to plunk her into one of those drive yourself carts at the grocery store. The ones reserved for disabled people."

"You're kidding?" Jaeda's nose was starting to get sore from pinching it, so he pushed his hand under his leg. Was Rob really serious? Or, was he putting him on?

"Sorry." Rob paused again. "It does get better, or, at least different." Jaeda heard a throat clearing, then, "Did she call her doctor? Just to be sure?"

"Called this morning. We were both on the line. 'Welcome to impending fatherhood,' the nurse said with a chuckle. I wanted to smack her. Glad I wasn't in the office in front of her."

"Me, too, bud. Cindy isn't here, or I would put her on. She could call you or Con back later."

Jaeda placed the phone receiver down quietly. His cubicle office was surrounded with plexiglass dividers, but he didn't want other bank officers or employees to hear his private conversation. Most were respectful, but Amber Adams sometimes hovered near his desk as she passed trying to look intent on her cellphone. She always turned quickly to him and winked. Maybe okay for friends, but was she really one? He remembered that right after he and Connie moved to Scottsdale. Amby, as she liked to be called, invited him to lunch at 92nd Street Café, just a stone's throw from the office. He was uncomfortable and gave a lame excuse to check on Connie. Amby hadn't entirely bought it, but reached out and tweaked his nose. She started to pass by now, then paused and grinned at him. She was cute in her own way. Sort of boyish with a clipped haircut and always wearing men-type shirts. Very flirtatious.

"Home troubles, bro?" He hated when she called him that. It sounded a bit racist. Although he knew Candy called her brother Billy "Bro." Different. Not in a professional setting, and Billy is white.

His conversation with Rob encouraged him. "Please do not ever address me that way again." There, he'd said it; what he'd wanted to say for months. He watched her eyebrows form triangles and her blue eyes turn dusky and dark. She reached out to tweak his nose, and he put his hand up to stop her like a traffic cop. "No! Do not touch me."

Jaeda was humming a tune he made up on his drive home. What he didn't expect was their little dog Jake whining on the floor next to a prone Connie.

Connie moaned and Jake whimpered looking to Jaeda for help. Jaeda picked up her overly bulky frame embracing his hands around her extended belly. She was breathing, but moaning. A sigh escaped her lips. "Jaede, need you. Sorry." Why was she apologizing? Should he call 911? He lifted her and carried her to the bedroom and laid her gently on the fluffy down comforter. Her fingers twitched and her legs trembled. His stressed mind recalled them dancing at the Pavilion in Newport Beach, delighting in each other and starting to fall in love.

"What happened, Con? Can you tell me?"

No response. An almost quiet snuffling – not really a snore. Jaeda ran to the medicine cabinet and grabbed a thermometer. He remembered how to take a pulse and put his fingers on her wrist. Shoving the thermometer under her tongue he held it there for a full minute. It was one of those that beeped when the temp was recorded. 99.08 – almost normal. That was when he heard her moan again.

"Scared. Tripped. Fell on baby."

Connie was almost five months pregnant. Jaeda caressed her belly. The baby was doing aerobics big time. He could even see the big balloon, as he called it, moving sideways and up and down.

"Thirsty." Good sign, he hoped. Little Jake jumped on the bed and snuggled between Connie's legs while he went to the kitchen for a glass of water.

Chapter Six
Cindy
Decision

Cindy almost screamed at Rob. "You didn't tell me?" She had just gotten home from praying with neighbors.

Rob mumbled. "Thought I reassured him. Not that big of deal. I have been through it with you."

Cindy slammed the door behind her, loudly. The sound of the wobbly screen made her feel better. Little Robby was asleep; she had been visiting with a young couple who were having a lot of problems – marriage, relocating and parents. She hoped they would attend the next church meeting, especially the couples Bible study in their house. House that it is. A bungalow, as the local people called it, on stilts. Where she had been raised in the Midwest USA, a bungalow was a low, one story home with a lot of grass and a garage. In a middle-class neighborhood.

In Playa Hermosa, Costa Rica it was very different. It was on the beach. Where Rob could surf every day to strengthen his muscles and relieve his tension.

She stomped down the rickety stairs. She knew she needed her Lord, but she was angry. Frustrated. She and Rob had spent so many months, over a year, trying to establish a church congregation on this lonely beach in Costa Rica. Robby, their precious son had been born here, but other than that, not much had happened. Nothing significant.

Cindy pulled at her sun-bleached hair and her flimsy cotton top. *What is happening, Lord, or not happening? I know you sent us here. I know You provided for us with the missionary subsidies from church, but not much is happening here.* She remembered a passage from her morning devotions that always inspired and comforted her. Psalm 31:15 said it all. "*My times are in your hand.*"

She wandered onto the beach, the pristine white sand beach where she and Rob had married. It had been spectacular. Everyone who loved them had attended. Her dad and Rob's mother, Lydia, had lighted the unity candle; Ms. Dana's children practically danced down the aisle in fancy dresses, except for Shayden the boy twin and his cousins, Fletcher and Huxley, who performed as ring bearers. Nine-year-old Teagan had played the wedding march on the borrowed keyboard anchored in the sand. It had been such a fun wedding fulfilling her dreams. The waves had rolled in unusually quiet, singing their song of love and eternity.

Cindy kicked at the wet sand with her bare toes. Why, God, hadn't she and Rob been more successful in planting a church here in Playa Hermosa? She truly believed, no actually knew, He had guided them to this beautiful place. She missed her family, and she knew Rob missed his. She missed his, too. Little Robby didn't know the difference. Costa Rica was all he knew, but she wanted him to know his grandparents and aunts and uncles in the states. Could they afford to take him back there for a visit? Expensive, but so much cheaper than all of them coming here. Robby's first birthday was coming up soon, so why not?

~

Cindy and Rob stood in line. In order to take baby Robby to the states they needed to verify his dual citizenship and update his passport. So much was slow in Costa Rica, so much red tape. Finally, it was their turn. Holding the precious papers, they sat in their car and prayed. How Cindy wished Rob could come with them to California to visit their parents. Finances wouldn't allow it. At least the grandparents and Candy Canes could meet Robby and celebrate his birthday.

~

Cindy stood by the baggage carrousel holding a squirming Robby against her shoulder. Where was Dad? He had promised to meet her. She saw her suitcases creeping around on the carrousel belt, one with her clothes, one with Robby's essentials, and two empty ones. Those were the ones she would fill with delicacies and needed items from the states to take back to Costa Rica. Maybe she would buy a few beef filets for Rob who craved them. Her friend Laura told her that as long as the stickers on them said Product of USA, they would go through customs. Still, Laura said to watch the customs officials in Costa Rica to be sure they didn't confiscate those precious meats.

Finally, she heard a loud guffaw. "Didn't know it would be so hard to park." Her dad paused with tears in his eyes. "My precious first grandbaby. Hi, little buddy." He grabbed Robby from Cindy's arms, and to Cindy's relief, he cuddled with his grandpa. It was going to be okay. It was going to be good. She had made the right decision.

Cindy and Robby settled into the guest room in her father's house. She inhaled the lingering lavender scent her mother had used for years as a room spray and as a personal cologne. She had breathed it in on her dad's neck when he was embracing her. She'd heard Dad say he went to storage and retrieved the crib Cindy had used as a baby. Cindy knew it wasn't considered safe by today's standards, and if her mother was alive she would have poo-pooed it, but she clamped her lips tight and hugged him enthusiastically. She would be with Robby the whole time he was in the crib. After all, Cindy had survived the ancient crib, so why couldn't Robby?

She was just getting settled and feeling comfy and relaxed when Rob called. Something was terribly wrong; she could hear it in his voice, even after he said his hello and told her he loved her. Before she even knew the problem, she immediately began worrying about his MS and his commitment to sobriety. Where was her trust?

Rob gulped and explained in an unsteady voice.

An unexpected deluge of rain had flooded the basement area of their little home. They'd just started to remodel it to add a bedroom and bath, somewhere they could accommodate occasional guests, like Dad. Or, Braydon and Noelle. It was planned so anyone who visited could stay with them instead of an expensive hotel. Rob's voice was a bit wobbly. "Brian, the manager, remember him? He helped me, and got some of the landscape workers to help. It took hours of scooping up mud and sweeping wet dirt. A mess, but we saved it." Then he added with a lilt in his voice, "Several AA friends and two from my MS therapy group came by to help. They even brought pizza."

Cindy always worried when he got emotional. Still, she reminded herself, it was part of the deal of being in AA and having a debilitating disease like multiple sclerosis. Rob was a strong man physically, and he had a strong faith. How could her dream man be anything else?

She hung up the landline phone and blew out a sigh of relief. Selfishly, she was glad she hadn't been there during the flooding. Those situations often harbored disease born bacteria from stagnant water. Robby could have gotten sick, or she and Rob could have. She hoped he and all the helpers had taken precautions and worn face masks. Praying a thank you praise she joined her dad at the TV. He was watching a stock car race she thought she'd have no interest in. However, it was entertaining. Inspired by his enthusiasm, she got caught up in it. Racing wildly around a track in cool cars sounded like fun. Maybe a release from tension.

Chapter Seven
Doreen
A Request

Melanie stirred her coffee and let Lola lick a taste of creamer off her finger. She swore the dog smiled at her again. She cuddled the funny looking critter who lapped at her chin. She pulled back and swaddled Lola into her arms. Lola's warmth was comforting, but Melanie wished for more.

Where was a Prince Charming for her? Did God plan for her to go into a convent? Be a spinster? She shook her head hard feeling her soft brown strands swishing on her cheeks. She swept them back with her fingers. She was only twenty-eight. And a half, she reminded herself, like a kid who states her age in halves to make herself look more mature, older. How silly. Not being good at math, she had almost failed it in sixth grade, she still sometimes counted on her fingers. Seven more years during which she could reproduce. Maybe more, but she wasn't clear about the latest studies. Did studies matter? She bowed her head to pray when the phone rang.

"Need you."

"Doreen?"

"Need to talk."

"Sure, but why me?"

"You and Nat are the only ones unencumbered – like not married. Need to pick your beautiful brain."

Melanie felt her sigh leap across the phone lines. What could she possibly tell Doreen?

Doreen prattled on about Bill, Jr. Hard to relate to that situation, but Melanie tried.

"He's gorgeous, a super model on his own. Even internationally." Her words choked out in a gargled sob. Melanie gripped the phone tighter. How could she help Doreen? She was a preschool teacher, not involved in modeling like Doreen, and definitely not in super modeling.

Melanie couldn't believe what Doreen was asking.

"I … I can't do that, Dor."

"Why not?"

Melanie hit the red button on her phone. How could she do what Doreen asked?

Melanie fiddled with her cellphone. Should she call Doreen back and apologize? She couldn't imagine doing what Doreen asked. Calling Bill Lord, Jr. was out of the question. Wasn't it? She had an innate fear of motorcycles. How would it help if she asked to ride his? Made no sense. Doreen hadn't made much either.~

Doreen slammed her phone down. She hadn't

made sense to Melanie. Didn't really explain. Yet, asked a lot. All she wanted was confirmation. Does Bill really love her, even with her gimpy leg? After all, she is a prominent model on the L.A. circuit. Her name is in many newspapers, mostly because she models clothes for women with disabilities. Did that count? She believed in it, and knew she was very blessed. Was she up to their relationship? Was Bill? Maybe she should call Melanie back. Confusion was not her usual state of mind.

~

Nat heard her buzzing phone. Maybe it was Larry. She hoped he would call and ask for a real date. She bit her lip and picked up the phone. Instead, she heard Doreen's trembling voice. Even with her shorter leg and obvious disability, Doreen always exuded confidence. She was tall, stately and eloquent. She had what Connie, her designer, called "a presence." She had stood out many times on runways showing flair and an over the top life confidence. She had inspired so many people, not just those with disabilities, but others with low self-esteem. She had almost become an icon. What was wrong with Doreen?

Chapter Eight
Jaeda and Connie
Too much help?

Jaeda insisted being in the room while the doctor examined Connie. After all, he was the father to be. Connie gripped his hand tightly while lying on the table with her feet in the cold metal stirrups. He turned his head when she said, "Ouch," and focused on the wall art of endangered animals. At least the doctor loved animals.

The doctor raised her head and looked directly at Jaeda. "She's fine, babies are fine. Sorry you had a scare. She nodded toward Jaeda, "babies in the womb this far along are very resilient." She grinned, held a piece of paper out to Jaeda and clasped his hand. Everything was going to be fine. Wasn't it? What had the doctor said? Babies? Plural. No, couldn't be.

Jaeda was relieved that Dr. H. gave Connie a good

bill of health. He had been worried about the baby, Little X, as he called it. Connie wasn't quite ready to learn the baby's gender, so he had honored that, even though the suspense was nagging at him. He couldn't figure out why she felt that way since she loved to decorate and design clothes, her profession. He had visions of yards of fabric in pinks or blues. Instead, the few yards she had draped over the ecru crib waiting to be cut and sewn were yellow. Fine for either sex, just so generic. He was sure the doctor had made a slip of tongue when she said "babies" plural. Hadn't she?

~

He whistled as he pushed the button to close the garage door and almost hopped into the house slamming the screen door behind him. "Connie, Con," he called wondering where she was. Usually, she came to the door to hug him and ask about his day. Like, "Did you meet any fun people today? Any celebrities?" So many, especially sports icons, lived in Scottsdale, and he had interacted with them helping with their credit card accounts and other bank issues. Today there was silence.

"Jake? Jakey, boy?" Odd. The little dog always greeted him at the door and ran in circles barking at his heels. Now he was worried. When he heard a moan from the sofa, he was scared.

~

"She what?" Connie's sister Sandra almost yelled in his ear. Jaeda held the phone away and up high. Gosh, that woman could react. Yet, he was grateful for the next words she spoke.

"I will see if Mom and Dad can watch the kids

and come right away. Call you later."

Jaeda wasn't sure what to do. Connie had asked for Sandra, not one of her Candy Cane sisters. Usually, those six, now seven with Melanie, stuck together like fleas on a hound. But, he reflected, family aced. Sandra, he remembered, was the one who supported Connie marrying outside of her race, to him. She was the one who somehow made it okay and acceptable to their parents. He would pick her up at Sky Harbor Airport tomorrow on his day off.

After just a year plus of marriage, Jaeda knew he must call at least one of the Candy Canes. It was a given, considering how close they all were. He chose Melanie. Not sure why. She and Nat seemed to have the most job flexibility, and because she taught preschool and got off work a little after three, he knew he could reach her.

"She what?" Melanie seldom yelled that he knew of, she was usually soft spoken and logical. Again, he held the phone up high. "Have you taken her to that physical therapy place Nat went to?"

"Spine Scottsdale?"

"Yes, that one."

"Her doctor recommended it."

"For gosh sakes, Jaede, call for an appointment. Tell them it's an emergency. I will alert the others." Then she hung up.

~

"Men!" Why were men so dense? Getting Connie in for physical therapy would have been the first thing Melanie would have done, especially since her obstetrician recommended it. Waiting was not an option, at least for her. She called Natalie who had the California link to the Costa Rica number for Cindy, and soon had all the other girls were on group dial up.

~

Jaeda wished Val, his Sissy, could be here, too. He needed support. Rob was the only other husband he felt close to, not even his colleagues at the bank. Well, maybe Bill, Sr. who was like a father to all of them when he married Candy's widowed mom, Vivian. He called Bill.

~

Bill coughed as he picked up the phone. This seasonal cold was nagging at him. When he stopped hacking, he could finally listen. With a tissue in hand squeezing his nose, he understood Jaeda's words, sort of. He wondered why Jaeda hadn't called the Candy Canes. Then the other man reassured him he had. What did Jaeda want with him, old coot Bill?

Another coughing episode came on, so he passed the phone to Vivian.

Bill heard her offer to fly to Scottsdale to be a temporary mom to Connie. What was she thinking? He needed her here in Newport to attend to his cold. Who would prop him up at night and place the hot cloth of Vick's Vaporub on his chest and hand him a cup of herbal tea? He went to their bedroom to lie down and suffer alone.

~

Jaeda rested the phone in its socket on the kitchen counter. Bill sounded awful. Vivian was a trooper offering to come to Arizona to help. He questioned why he had called. Desperation? Needing an older male to assure him? He heard Connie moaning again, and Jake snuffling. Time to be a big man.

Maybe flowers would help. He hated to leave her alone, but she had Jake to comfort her and she was snoring softly. Throwing on his jacket to ward off the evening chill, he sprinted to his car and raced to North Scottsdale Floral where he had bought the gorgeous bouquet for Connie when she announced their pregnancy. It was almost five, and he worried he wouldn't make it in time. He pulled up to the last parking spot just as he saw a young woman closing the door and hanging the Closed sign in the window. Forgetting to lock his car, he banged on the glass door hoping he looked pleading enough. Marg, who he recognized as the owner, waved her hand to the girl. He could read her lips, "Let him in."

Jaeda walked out with three bouquets. One for Connie, one for her sister Sandra and one for Vivian. Hopefully they would show his gratefulness and cheer Connie up.

Chapter Nine
Melanie
A Dare

Melanie was perplexed. Why had Jaeda called her? Instead of Cindy or Natalie, or even Noelle who was recently pregnant? She decided to not reflect on it. Maybe for some reason her number came up first on the Candy Cane list. He had asked her to contact all the others, even mentioned something about her being organized and logical. She wished.

Frustrated maybe, but not logical. If she were, she would have figured out why Doreen was asking her to do a crazy thing. Doreen was the Candy Cane sister that had encouraged her to do the swim test that gave her entry into the group. Not that it was exclusive, exactly, but it was made up of six girls from a winning competitive team. She supposed, at least at the beginning, she was welcomed as a gesture of kindness. Especially by Doreen whose accident she had caused. Now, she was perhaps closer to Natalie than any of the others. Yet, she loved them all, and they all showed love and friendship to her. She rubbed her hands along her arms and leaned in to Lola for a sloppy kiss. It was special to be part of a loving group. She picked up her phone again and called the number for Bill, Jr. that Doreen had given her. Maybe he wouldn't answer and she could leave a message.

~

Bill, Jr. hung up the phone. Melanie? Strange. She had never called him before, although he knew her as one of the special friends. He felt confused. Why had Melanie said Doreen suggested she call him? Scared of riding a cycle? Wanting to get over it? With him?

He remembered Melanie being attractive with long fluffy brown hair. Nice girl, sort of cute in a wholesome way. Not his dream like Doreen. He wanted to honor the girl he loved, Doreen. Strange she hadn't alerted him about Melanie's call. Oh, well, it might be fun to share an experience on a cycle with a frightened girl. Maybe he could help her "get over it," as she mentioned in a shaky voice. He would try.

~

Melanie wore tight jeans and a warm jacket. Was that right? She clasped Bill, Jr.'s hand firmly and threw a leg over the back of the cycle as he instructed. Gripping her arms around his torso didn't seem right, but he told her to do it. "Hold on tight," he said in a loud voice over the rumble of the cycle. They were off!

The feeling was exhilarating, freeing. The plastic thing over her eyes on the borrowed helmet kept them from dirt and dust, and she could actually see. The bouncing up and down was a bit disconcerting at first, but it felt kind of good, like jumping up and down at a concert. This was a concert of sorts, wasn't it? Maybe she could get used to this.

Melanie was shaking. The motorcycle ride with Bill, Jr. was exciting, but her body wasn't used to all the jolting. Skydiving she could do floating in air, but riding a cycle? She filled her tub with very hot water and half a bottle of Victoria's Secret bubble bath. She drifted off sinking into its comfort and dreamed about a tall, muscular man with a deep laugh that made his baby blues sparkle. Doreen was chasing him, running after him, but the roar of his Harley blotted out her screams. Melanie stood on the sidewalk waving to Bill. Why didn't he come back to pick her up?

She coughed when bubbles filled her nose. Spitting out perfumed water, she pulled the plug. What had she been thinking? Bill was off limits. What had Doreen been thinking? It was obvious to Melanie that Bill was enamored with her stately model friend. He'd told Mel at least three times he was giving her the cycle ride because Doreen requested it. Hello, Doreen!

~

Doreen tried Mel's cellphone three times. Where was that girl? She should be back now from the cycle ride. She hoped Bill and Mel hadn't had an accident, or worse, kissed. Maybe her little ploy had been too over the top? She thought back to high school Shakespeare class and Romeo and Juliet. Was she really that insecure? Yep, she was. She jumped in her car and drove to Melanie's. Mel answered the door in bare feet and a huge fluffy robe with a big towel wrapped around her head. Was she alone?

Doreen felt like a fool. Although Melanie pulled her in and settled her on the sofa with a cup of freshly brewed coffee, she didn't feel right. What had she been thinking not trusting Melanie, Bill, and her own heart? Why had she called Melanie to play matchmaker? She had forgiven her a long time ago for causing the accident that injured her leg. As Cindy would say, God provided with an amazing plan. Doreen had had a menial retail job then, but now, thanks to the accident and Connie she was a celebrated model. Her talent and Connie's designs had elevated them both to acclaim. Would that have transpired if the accident hadn't happened? She wasn't sure. She trusted her Candy Cane sisters and her Lord. Why did she question?

She sipped the wonderful coffee and held Melanie's hand. Maybe it was time to let go of uncertainty and confusion. Maybe time to trust and relax. She turned her face toward Melanie and noticed the sparkle in her eyes.

"He was nice, courteous and kind. He only talked about you, girl. You are the one."

Mel looked directly into Doreen's blanched face. "He adores you. More than loves. Adores. Do you get that?"

Chapter Ten
Vivian
Helping Connie

Vivian Lord kissed Bill, Sr. goodbye on his forehead and jumped on the little cycle he had given her as a wedding gift. She would ride it on back streets to the airport, then take a plane. Hadn't Bill her hubby told her to be fearless? Her clothes flapped around her, her auburn hair specked with gray flew in the wind, and she felt free. At almost seventy it was an exhilarating experience. Bill would be fine she convinced herself. Kirstin Day and Lydia Lovejoy and daughter Candy had all offered to look after him. He would be fine. Even son Billy would check in on him. It was only a seasonal cold.

She pulled up and parked in the Orange County Airport covered lot, locked the cycle and grabbed her floppy valise. This, she decided, would be a fun adventure. She had never been to Scottsdale before, and she loved taking care of people. She would take care of Connie who she loved almost as a daughter, a Candy Cane sister to her own daughter Candy. They would have a great time together. After all, she was an experienced mom who could deal with anything. She trotted toward Gate Four and stood in the security line.

~

Jaeda didn't know what to do. Two women were insistent on coming to help Connie. Where would each stay? He remembered they had that pop-up bed tucked in the closet in Connie's work room. He would have to fold up the crib and move her drawing table aside to get to it. It would take up a lot of room in the crowded space, but it could work. He opened the closet door and dragged it out. Connie was napping on the sofa, so he hoped she hadn't heard him. She would want to organize and instruct. She needed rest. Tomorrow he would call Spine Scottsdale for an appointment for her. She hadn't even seen the gorgeous bouquet. Maybe when she woke up. Jake snoozed between her legs, so he knew she was protected.

He stuck the other two bouquets in glasses of water in the kitchen sink. Maybe he was premature buying them today. However, when he picked up Sandra and Vivian tomorrow from Sky Harbor Airport, he would have a welcoming burst of color for each. His hands shook as he wheeled the popup bed from the closet. Why was he so nervous? Partly, he knew, worrying about Connie, but also dealing with an anxious sister-in-law and a pseudo mother. Both had accepted him as Connie's husband, very graciously. Both were white. Would that make a difference? He pushed the doctor's careless word out of his head. He'd heard she delivered a lot of twins, so using the plural was just habit.

~

Jaeda stood outside of Gate 6 at Sky Harbor Airport. His arms were filled with flowers. Both women were coming in close to the same time. That, he surmised, was a blessing. He didn't have to drive there twice. Sky Harbor was now one of the busiest in the states, not like smaller John Wayne Orange County Airport in Newport Beach. He spied Sandra first lugging a carryon in maroon. She squealed and threw her arms open to embrace him.

Fifteen minutes later Vivian Lord bounced next to them. They were waiting in the baggage claim area chatting when she bounded up and laughed. "Came to the rescue!"

Jaeda and Sandra looked askew at each other. He opened his mouth to explain, but the words choked his throat. Sandra sent him an evil look. Hadn't he told her Vivian was coming, too?

Vivian saved the day, or at least the moment. "You must be the wonderful sister, Sandra." The younger woman nodded and pasted a plastic smile on her face. "I," Vivian explained, "am the honorary Candy Cane mom. You know about the Candy Canes?"

Sandra nodded again. "I know Connie is one of them. Who are you to them?"

"I am Candy's mom. I married Bill Senior two years ago. Remember?"

"Sort of," Sandra nodded. "I don't understand

why you are here."

"It is what I do. The mom thing."

"Oh."

"I want to take the stress off you. I will be here to take over when you need a break. Okay?"

"I guess. I'm here to help Connie, my sister."

"Of course you are, dear. Even you will need a few moments alone to regroup. I can take those. I will not get in your way."

"Oh, that's nice. Thank you."

"Maybe we could take shifts."

Sandra looked at Vivian like she had three heads, as if what was with this woman? Much older than her own mother.

Jaeda drove the women home and worried all the way about sleeping arrangements. That was the least of his worries. When he walked in dragging Sandra's suitcase and Vivian's valise, Connie started yelling. "I don't want all these people here. I'm a big girl. I'm fine." Her voice escalated, and little Jake started to whimper. What had changed her mind?

~

Vivian claimed the popup bed. She felt like a proverbial fifth wheel. Why had she insisted on coming? She had never stopped to think, even ask, if Connie had family coming to help. Recently, she had become more spontaneous. Since she had been married to Bill Lord, Sr. Was that because of Bill, or *because* of Bill? Lately, they had butted horns. Not big issues, but little incidental ones. Like who was responsible for getting the cars washed; or, which of them should decide what salad to eat for dinner. Stupid stuff. "You decide."

"No, you. It's your turn."

The small meaningless arguments echoed in her head. She refused to let them invade her heart.

She unpacked the few items of clothing she had jammed into her carryon, shook them out, refolded them and shoved them into the two small drawers next to her popup bed. This would do. She wouldn't be staying long, just long enough to help. Why was Connie so belligerent? Hopefully, hormones. Pregnancy does that to some women. Did it to her when she was carrying Billy. Not when she was pregnant with Candy. Mmm. Maybe Connie will have a boy. Jaeda would be thrilled, but she suspected he would adore his child of any sex. Then she had a random thought. Would color matter?

Connie pulled the afghan on the sofa up higher to her chin. The fringe tickled and she sneezed. Who were all these people, and why were they here? Jaede must have invited them. She forced herself to prop up lifting her belly with both hands. "Why are you all here?"

Sandra leapt up from the table where they were having dinner, takeout that Jaeda had provided. She wrapped her arms around Connie and hugged so hard Connie winced. "What? You asked me to come."

Connie looked spaced out. Her eyes searched the funky chandelier over the dining table. "I did?"

"Yes. Jaeda called me. You asked for me. You don't remember?"

Chapter Eleven
Natalie
Plans

Natalie had tried to call Melanie twice. How had the cycle ride with Bill, Jr. gone? Dying to know was not a random thought. She closed up the gym for the night and started to punch a number in her cell. Now, why did she do that? Stupid, Nat. If the man was interested he would have called. Larry hadn't.

It had been well over a week since their arranged meeting at Starbucks. Was she so desperate? Maybe. She wished Doreen had asked her to ride with Bill, Jr. instead of Melanie. Oops. Now she sounded jealous, even to herself. Yep, she was desperate.

~

Larry hesitated with his finger hovering over his cell. He was back in Arizona at his security guard job, but since it was a small community with few cars coming in that didn't have the Community sticker on them, he had a lot of time to ruminate. Or, he chuckled, waste.

When he came in at six a.m. he'd gritted his teeth at all the crumbs on the guard house floor. Instead of crunching through them and messing up his clean shoes, he got out the broom and dustpan. Why were the late evening and night guards so careless? How hard would it have been to stuff cookies in their mouths over the trash can? Guess they hadn't been raised the same as him.

He just finished wiping the counters and the inside of the windows when the security company mail courier pulled up. He helped unload the crates and immediately started sorting the mail. As he put bills and ads and random flyers in residents' boxes he noticed several for the Waymans. Jaeda and Connie were favorites, the ones who trusted him and recommended him for the PI job to follow Bryce that took him from Arizona to California and Las Vegas and back to Arizona, then to Newport Beach to meet Natalie. Maybe the trust thing shouldn't have happened. Too late now. If he were a praying man, he would have asked for forgiveness.

His fingers stopped hovering.

He called.

Natalie stared at her phone. Larry? After all this time? Maybe she should ignore and let it go to voicemail. Nope, not good at patience. When she heard his voice, her heart couldn't stop pounding. Could he hear it?

"I have a free weekend and thought it might be fun to get together. Anything special happening in Newport?"

"Always. Let's see," she paused holding her hand over a pounding heart. "Looking through the articles in Stu News, an online newspaper that highlights local events." She tried unsuccessfully to stifle a giggle. "There are always whale watching excursions. There's a bridal show." She giggled again. "Oh, there's a car show every Sunday afternoon with a free raffle and free donuts. There are also cruises on John Wayne's former yacht The Wild Goose to celebrate his birthdate. That might be fun. You would get to see a lot of the famous old movie star's homes. There's always something." She held her breath. "When can you come?"

"I can't leave until after six, and would arrive around midnight. Or, could meet you in morning."

What would she do with him at midnight? Couldn't stay with her, but maybe Vivian and Bill, Sr.'s. They had an extra room since Candy had married Devin again. Or, maybe Billy in Dana Point. Even the Lovejoy's or the Day's. So many options. How would each accept a handsome man of color? She almost started dialing, but needed to confer with Melanie first. She finally got her.

"Why are you so stressed, girl? So far, he is just a friend, and no one in our circle, parents included, have any problem with people of color," as you put it." Melanie's snicker burst into a full-blown laugh. "Maybe you should call Jaeda for his take on this."

Natalie put down the phone feeling humbled. Melanie was so right. Maybe she would call Jaeda. He would reassure her.

When he answered, she could hardly hear his voice for all the chattering in the background. Lots of laughing, too. She held the phone away from her ear until Connie's sweet voice came on. Although, it wasn't so sweet as usual. The "What? Who is this?" The confrontational tone really set her off.

"Me, Con. Nat. You okay?"

Natalie was disturbed to learn Connie was having troubles with her pregnancy. Mostly, she was told, about falling. Connie's back hurt, and she had an appointment with Spine Scottsdale Physical Therapy where Nat had gone after her sky diving accident. Nat remembered how attentive they were. She was glad Connie was going there. She hadn't known they did PT on pregnant women. Guess she was always learning.

Chapter Twelve
Jaeda
Confusion

A cute redhead, Heather, behind the reception desk said, "Welcome to Spine Scottsdale." Then she handed Connie a clipboard with several pages to fill out. Jaeda guided Connie to a chair in the waiting area. Heather's eyebrows raised dramatically. She must have noticed that Connie was very pregnant. She looked to Katie, maybe for help? The other woman nodded and stood to guide Connie to a private room.

"Shane will evaluate you," she said kindly. Connie lumbered up holding Jaeda's hand. The two settled in chairs opposite from Shane Sullivan, Director. He nodded to them, smiled and started asking questions. Finally, they were back in the reception area.

"Well, that went well," Jaeda said smiling at his

Connie.

"I felt intimidated. He asked so many personal questions."

"Like what? He simply asked how you felt, where you hurt and how did it happen?"

"I felt like a fool telling him I tripped over one of Jake's toys. Like an old woman who needs a walker."

Jaeda took her face in his hands, his fingers caressed her cheeks. His bottomless brown eyes almost sunk into her blue ones. He pulled her close feeling her extended belly pressing into his hips. He felt the movement of a child, his child and Connie's. He needed to reassure her and get their lives back on track. "Con, this is not about you, or us. It's about our baby. Yes, it is about you that you will feel better. You need to find a way to do that for the baby's sake." He looked around; all the women at the front desk had their heads bowed. Praying? He hoped.

Wrapping his arms around her, he led her to the recliner chair a young woman named Martina gestured to. He watched as Connie had a hot wrap put on her back and little pads placed on her leg, a pillow behind her head and the foot rest of the chair lifted. Wow, looked comfy to him. Maybe he could get some physical therapy, too, for stressed fathers-to-be.

While he was sitting in the waiting area, he caught whispered chatter from the females behind reception desk.

"She's so pretty," Michelle said.

"She's a clothing designer, has a boutique in

California."

"I heard her husband used to be one of her models." Giggle.

"Naw, he's a banker."

"Wonder how they met. Probably not at the bank."

Just then a slim, striking blonde with a pony tail approached Jaeda. "Are you Connie's husband?" she asked in a soft voice. He nodded.

"Is something wrong?"

"Not at all. I'm Emily Sullivan, Shane's wife. I come in to help occasionally, so I will be chatting with Connie. Shane forgot to ask about the babies' due date."

Another slip of tongue? He felt his mouth drop open and his clasped hands shake together. "Babies?"

"Yes. It's pretty obvious she is carrying two. I'm no expert, but I have given birth to four and learned a lot." Emily looked sideways at him. "You look surprised," she said. "Even shocked."

Jaeda felt the blood drain from his face. He looked up at Emily from his chair. Her face looked puzzled. What did his look like?

"Surely," she said, "your obstetrician told you. You must have had an ultra sound."

"She did. I wasn't there. She wanted to go alone." He shook his head. "I'm sorry I didn't insist." He gazed at this kind woman who knew more about his wife than he did. "Why wouldn't she have told me?"

"I don't have the answer for that, unless the technician made a mistake, inexperienced ones sometimes do. Or," she closed her eyes in thought, "maybe your wife wanted to surprise you?"

Jaeda fiddled with his thumbs. What was going on? Had Connie known and deceived him? He heard some commotion and stood up from his chair. Three attendants were guiding Connie to a physical therapy table. "She can't lie on her stomach." The others laughed, and Connie did, too. They seated her upright with her legs hanging over the side. Shane Sullivan slipped on a pair of clear plastic gloves. What was he going to do to his precious Connie?

Emily must have noticed his concern. "Shane is going to gently massage her back," she said. "It's called one of the modalities, helps to relax the muscles." She paused when he nodded. "After the message, Leanne will give her ultrasound on her leg, the one that keeps buckling. Then, Alexis will give her some short exercises in the gym. Jacob will finish with ice packs." She raised her blonde brows, maybe questioning if he understood.

~

Jaeda led Connie to the car and settled her in with the seatbelt extended to the max. She stared straight ahead. Nothing said, nothing gained.

Vivian rushed to the car when they pulled into the drive. "How are you, precious?" The woman exuded 'mommism.' Connie just nodded a bit and allowed Vivian to enfold her in her arms. Maybe she squeezed too tight because Connie winced. Still, it gave Jaeda a good feeling to know Connie was so loved.

Sandra hurried out next extending her arms with a scowl on her face. "My precious sister!" She barely glanced at Vivian, only long enough to glare.

Jaeda gripped Connie's elbow on one side, and Sandra on the other. Vivian "tch, tched" behind them. He knew his face was drawn and his eyes red-rimmed. There was a lot he still had to figure out. Like, twins?

Jaeda didn't know what to do. He had been blindsided about being a future parent to twins. First by his wife, then the doctor. Who could he trust? He called his mom.

"Honey," she said, "embrace this blessing. Stop ruminating over it. God always has a good plan."

His dad must have grabbed the phone. "Buck up, boy. Look at the blessings."

He put down his phone, releasing his only connection to those from whom he could get advice and security. He felt empty. He could hear the women fondering over Connie in the kitchen. He heard Connie laugh, although a bit brittle, it seemed to come from deep within her heart. Hope, that's what he needed, hope.

Jaeda tucked Connie into bed, snuggling her under the fluffy comforter. He pulled warm socks on her feet after rubbing them. What else could he do? He pulled her close and kissed her goodnight, but she didn't respond. Then, he prayed.

His mom called him the next morning. He'd almost not pushed the button to take it. But, when a grown man's mom calls … well, better answer.

"Gonna give some advice," she said in her no-nonsense voice. "You need to ditch your own concerns, deep six them. Yes, I mean that." She heard his groan, but ignored it and pressed on.

"Mom, you don't understand. She deceived me,

the doctor did, too. Maybe not quite the same, but I was clueless." He drew a deep breath. "About twins."

"So?"

That was all his mom could say? "So?"

Chapter Thirteen
Melanie
Idea

Melanie picked up Lola's deposit. That's what she felt like. Dog poo. She was still lonely, even with the sweet cuddly dog who she coaxed to run with her every morning and evening on the Back Bay. The scraggly looking dog was very obedient, always looked toward her for confirmation when her long snout wasn't glued to the terrain. She was such an alert dog that she sensed when cyclists and runners and even a bevy of baby ducks were near. There was one big Standard Black Poodle that Lola detested. Melanie often had to jerk lightly on her leash and say the "leave it" command the trainer had taught her.

Melanie tugged off her running socks, tossed them in the laundry basket and headed for the shower. The hot spray stabbed her skin, and she found herself sobbing. Was it for loneliness, or the baby she had lost years ago, or the fact she was a preschool teacher coddling and cuddling children she wished she could have as her own? Her mind drifted to the cycle ride with Bill, Jr. She would never impose on Doreen's happiness, but he is adorable. She rinsed the conditioner out of her hair squeezing tight. Maybe someday ... someday ... for her. When?

She dressed in the accepted preschool teacher attire, slacks and knit top, tennies. Would Nora be back? Would she be confrontational? Explain why she had left abruptly? Had Dana the director spoken with her? Would she ever find a love of her own?

~

Natalie was worried about Melanie. She was glad Mel had adopted the adorable dog, but would that be enough to comfort her? She was lonely, too, but at least she had her business. Nat's Gym took up a lot of hours. Her biggest frustration was finding another trainer since Bryce had become incognito. She slammed her fist down on her desk and scattered papers. Why hadn't she put everything online like Bill, Sr. had suggested? *I am living in the dark ages.* She scooped the papers off the floor and tried to organize them. An exercise in futility. Pulling a manila file folder from a drawer, she shoved the whole pile into it and labeled it TOMORROW. Maybe she and Mel could get together for something. Coffee?

Her heart wrenched when she heard Melanie's voice. She knew she had made the right call.

~

Melanie pulled out a chair at their favorite

Starbucks. Nat sauntered in and immediately asked, "You mind if we sit outside? One table left, and it's such a lovely evening."

"Guess that's okay." Melanie picked up her cup and followed Nat.

"I've been cooped up all day in my office at the gym. Not even a Zumba class to relieve the boredom.

So, how's it going with Lola? Is she running with you every morning?"

Melanie nodded with wet eyes. "She's still a doll, but she can't fill the loneliness." She hesitated and looked up at Nat whose eyes were blinking rapidly. "Gonna ask you a loaded question." Nat nodded her okay.

"Have you ever looked at the online dating websites?"

Chapter Fourteen
Melanie and Natalie
Searching for Love

They were having so much fun.

"Look at this guy. Trying to look like a stud, forcing muscles he doesn't have."

Laughing, Natalie collapsed her forehead on Melanie's kitchen table. Viewing potential dates, even on Christian dating websites, left her in a laugh puddle. Was she, even Melanie, that desperate? She asked the question. Mel nodded yes.

That sent them off in giggles again. Until the next guy popped up.

"Gosh, he's gorgeous! No," Melanie said, "he can't be a Christian."

"Why? You don't think handsome men are Christians? Or Christian men are handsome?"

"Maybe they lie. I couldn't deal with that, with lies."

"Maybe they didn't. Mel, you have to trust. This website with putting in things you like to do, and even the one that is Brunch Only seems safe. What's to lose if you join the first guy's running group once or twice? Or, have lunch with a man who is a CEO? Or, who likes your profile? Come on, girl, take a risk. God will protect your back."

They finally settled on two guys, one for each. One from the Christian website and one from the Brunch Only site. Melanie giggled as she made a suggestion for her first date, at Starbucks of all places. Of course, she and almost all the Candy Canes, had a relationship history there. Next time she stepped up to the counter she would ask about buying stock.

She wondered about the man; did he like her profile or her hair or the fact she loved to run every morning? He agreed to meet her next Saturday at Starbucks, outside, he specified, on the tables bordering crowded Pacific Coast Highway in Corona del Mar. Maybe he was looking for a quick excuse to run away. She would bring Lola, so if he did run, she wouldn't look so alone.

Natalie was conflicted. Brunch Only sounded good, not a big commitment. Who would pay? When B.J. responded, she felt confused. He suggested meeting at Sherman Gardens. It was a favorite of hers. Most guys wouldn't think of eating there. The fare was very much like having tea in an English garden. Tiny sandwiches, microscopic salad on the side, iced tea. Desserts were finger-sized. Was he gay? He did say the meal was on him. That part was encouraging. Perhaps an old-fashioned gentleman.

His picture had been fuzzy. Maybe not a great photo? He did look cute, and buff, and his smile, what she could see of it so far away, was engaging, seemed genuine.

~

Melanie wiggled into the last chair in front of Starbucks and looped Lola's leash around a table leg. Was her hair right? Her makeup? She had taken such care to make it look natural, but with a little embellishment. Suddenly, Lola stood up and wiggled.

Natalie fingered the silverware in the Sherman Foundation Gardens alfresco dining courtyard. She looked around at the beautiful foliage and colorful flowers wishing she knew more about them. She had heard they were all indigenous, native to Southern California. The pinks and blues filled her visual senses. Maybe she should take a tour sometime. After all, Noelle and Braydon had had their beautiful wedding here, and he was a rose expert for the garden. Cindy and Rob had met here, too, dancing after Noelle and Braydon's wedding. It was certainly an enchanted place, a place for love.

She finally placed the stiffly ironed napkin on her lap and smoothed it out. How long would he take to get here? Trust was a big issue for her, especially after the Bryce incident when he left her injured after her free fall sky dive. He never admitted to it. She couldn't dwell on the past. This was the future, maybe a good and fun one for her. Maybe marriage.

"Hi, Nat." She looked up into intense blue eyes the color of indigo and almost fainted. Waving her hand and the linen napkin over her face with a fervor, she caught her breath. Her hands were clammy, and she felt her body sinking into the chair. What was Bryce doing here?

He was deceiving her again.

~

"His name was?" Nat asked the question, Melanie responded scrunching up her nose.

"Nice guy. Not a super dog fan. He ignored Lola. She hungered down and whined. He kept asking why she was doing that. Hello, idiot, she wants attention. His name was George. Not that it matters."

Melanie felt her eyes bulge when Nat told her about her date.

"He really did that? Deceived you again? Played you for a fool? Do you trust him?"

"I have conflicted feelings. I want to trust him, but it's hard. I guess I always had feelings for him, not really romantic, but friend feelings. Does that make sense?"

"What about the Larry guy? You seemed to like him a lot."

"Yep, like him, even attracted to him. Just don't see a future with a wanderer."

Melanie glared at her. "You would have the same issues Connie had. A lot to overcome."

Melanie fidgeted with her skirt. She was wearing the blue flower one again with the God color on her knee. She moved it to place the best flower right on her kneecap. Wow, how stupid and superstitious was that? Not a Christian thing for sure. Natalie was worried, and she, Melanie, should help. How? She finally found her voice.

"How did he explain his coming to lunch with

you? What were his excuses for abandoning you before?"

"He didn't really. He acted almost as if this arranged meeting was a brand-new thing, almost as if we were new to each other." Nat paused to sniffle into a tissue, coughed and wiped one eye.

They were sitting on Melanie's lanai with a mini view of the Back Bay. The breeze ruffled their hair, and Melanie, now wearing her hair down from a ponytail, pushed the untidy brown strands behind her ears. Dusk was falling and the usual evening ocean clouds moved toward them. They were only a mile inland from the beach. The weather changed her mood. She remembered the old quip about being blessed to not live in rainy Seattle. Straightening her skirt once again, she reached for Natalie's hand and gripped hard.

She asked the question she had been toying with. "How do you feel about him now?"

Natalie tilted her chin up and raised her brows like two question marks. Melanie sensed her indecision and waited patiently for an answer. Finally, she asked again. "Yes?" She got the answer she expected.

"I don't know."

"Wanna elaborate?" Melanie was hopeful. She didn't want to press her friend, but she knew there was more.

"I still think he's cute; I still like him, sort of, because he was a very good trainer at my gym. Her eyes closed and she seemed to be searching for the words. "I can't stand ponytails on men! There, I've said it."

Melanie doubled over holding her stomach. Her laughter bubbled in the dusk. "That's it?"

Natalie nodded. Her face was crimson.

"After all he did, or didn't do, *that* is your reason for not liking him?"

"I guess. He is a great trainer, and the gym could really use him again. Still, he doesn't seem sincere."

"In what way?"

"He still didn't apologize, not even confess to leaving me on the ground after my sky diving accident. He never came to the hospital, didn't even so much as text "sorry.""

"That is a biggie. He has no remorse."

"Nope. And during our brief bunch situation, he never brought it up. I was so uncomfortable I didn't either. I should have. I was dumbfounded, just ate fast, thanked him and got up and left. I never acknowledged he was someone I knew, not just someone from the dating site. I feel so stupid."

Melanie couldn't resist the questions. "I have to ask. Did he pay?"

Natalie grinned almost gleefully and nodded.

Chapter Fifteen
Natalie
A Shoulder to Cry On

Natalie looked at her phone screen while her cell phone vibrated in her hand. Why had she kept Bryce's number on her contact list? She stuffed the phone in her purse, in its special pocket, and kept driving. It had been kind of fun going over the two mystery dates with Melanie, but she still felt empty and knew Mel did, too. Not that either had expected a big romance, but both were flops. At least Mel's was. What a jerk not even petting Lola who is such a sweet dog.

And what had Bryce hoped to accomplish by sneaking up on her? That's what she thought of his devious entrance – sneaking. She was sure he had known who she was. Her profile on the dating website would have revealed it very clearly to him. Gym owner; former sky diver; award winning swimmer; entrepreneur. What a jerk attempting to deceive her again. Even her initials and her moniker, Organized Girl, would have given it away. He knew. She knew he knew.

Suddenly, an SUV rounded the corner and jockeyed through the intersection too fast. She slammed on the brakes so hard her hands ached on the steering wheel. "Thank you, Jesus, that I avoided an accident. Please help me focus better on my driving, and please drive Bryce out of my head."

She was grateful she had such instant reflexes. Today they may have saved her life, or at least her little car. Ten years ago they gave her an edge to touch the end of the pool before her competitors. She had been a champion then, medaling with the other Candy Canes for over four years. Instead, she felt depleted. Her life was boring and routine. She was alone.

Maybe tomorrow she might confide in Claire, her alter ego at the gym. The woman was so intuitive. After all, hadn't she known that her son Nick and Emily the Feng Shui interior decorator, were perfect for each other? She had even arranged their unique wedding at Nat's Gym. Claire had surprised them all when she and Nick did the Mother and Son Dance. It had been the highlight of the reception. Natalie could still remember them hooting it up and dancing the Chicken, and Nick swinging his mom over his head. When the crazy dance ended, the guests snacked on mini hotdogs and jelly beans. She had adored all of the Candy Cane weddings – Noelle's at the famous Sherman Gardens, and Cindy's on the beautiful beach in Costa Rica, and Connie's to Jaeda at the historic Newport Pavilion. Even Candy's mother Vivian's to Bill Lord, Senior. She'd had the privilege of wearing a gorgeous gown designed by Connie for every wedding, and she had again worn one, though more unique, for Emily and Nick's wedding. That time it had been riotous with many colors, not just blue or pink or green satin and tulle to match the bride's eyes, but a rainbow of stripes and many colors blending into each other. The entire event was unique, very avant garde like Emily herself. If she ever had the blessing to marry her prince charming, she would have a wedding like that, one that was true to her personality, one that screamed Me, Natalie.

She pulled into her driveway and laid her forehead on the top of the steering wheel. What was she thinking? Romance and love were gifts for others. Not for her.

~

The next morning after a restless night, Natalie opened the gym at five. Just in case a few members were early birds. When Claire showed up, early as usual, she took the older woman's hand and practically dragged her into the small office.

Claire shook her head in bewilderment, then pulled out the uncomfortable wooden guest chair. Before Nat could speak, Claire said, "I want to buy a new chair. This one hurts my bottom. It will be a gift. Do you mind?"

Nat giggled slightly and nodded. "Thanks so much. It would be a treat."

Finally, Claire asked, "What's going on? You look . . . well, worried."

Natalie seldom bared her soul, but although she fought them, tears streamed down her face. Claire rose from the uncomfortable chair and swiftly embraced Natalie in her motherly arms. Nat's anguished sobs filled the small room.

"I am lost, a lost cause."

Chapter Sixteen
Larry
The Visit

Larry jumped off his cycle and silenced the rumbling motor. It was twelve minutes after midnight in a residential community. Although Natalie had reassured him he would be welcome, even late, he walked quietly up the flagstone to the extravagant house. He hesitated ringing the bell when suddenly the door swung open.

"You must be Larry, Nat's friend." It wasn't a question, more a greeting. He felt himself smile and clasped the warm hand of an older gentleman. Why he thought the man was a gentleman, he wasn't sure. Just knew.

Bill Lord pulled him inside a home filled with treasures. Larry looked around. No Picassos here, but photos of family and little objects obviously made by children.

"Thanks so much. Very welcoming place." Bill nodded, smiled. Larry felt out of sorts. He had never been in a home like this one. Simple furnishings, but filled with memories.

Bill as he was told to call him, said, "Just a sec. I will raise the garage door so you can park your cycle in there." Then, he disappeared. Larry stood mutely, waiting and looking around. His special cycle shoes scrunched in the depth of an Oriental carpet. The colors of it almost blew him away, until he noticed the frames of the many photos picked up the same colors. Bill returned and gestured for Larry to park his cycle in the third garage. Larry did and couldn't help but notice the BMW and Mercedes in the other two. And the Harley. There was a well-organized work bench with numerous tools hanging from a pegboard above it. Sitting on the work surface was an uncompleted wood carving; maybe a dog, or a bird? Hard to tell, but the shape was smooth and beautiful.

Wandering into the kitchen from the inside garage door, Larry pushed the big white button to close it and was greeted by a wide grin.

"I can offer you coffee, tea, homemade lemonade. Sorry, no beer in this house."

"Coffee would be great. It was a long drive."

Bill settled Larry at the kitchen counter, his favorite talking place. It's where he had talked with Bill, Jr. and Jaeda and his new son-in-law, Devin. "Sorry Vivian isn't here. She's in of all places Scottsdale helping to take care of Connie Wayman." Larry nodded. What was wrong with Mrs. Wayman?

"That's okay. I am grateful for you putting me

72

up." Then, he asked, "The Waymans are wonderful people. Actually," he paused, "they've become friends. I hope everything is all right with them."

Bill grinned. "Probably is now that Vivian is there. She is the ultimate mom."

Larry grinned back and nodded. He was glad Mrs. Connie, as he often called her, had help. "Is there a schedule I need to be aware of?"

"Nope. I usually make coffee on the timer before I go to bed, so it will be ready in the morning whenever." Bill paused. "I know you have plans with Natalie tomorrow." He hesitated. "Something special? I don't mean to pry."

When Larry didn't answer, burying himself in his coffee mug, Bill got up and led him to the guest room. Some things shouldn't always be shared.

~

Natalie opened the text.

I'm here! What time tomorrow?

How about breakfast at 9? My house or IHOP? You choose.

Larry couldn't resist seeing where she lived. So, he pulled up to her condo at 8:45, a bunch of Gerber Daisies in his hand.

She was stirring eggs in a large skillet. He smelled bacon, and maybe sausage. She pulled a simple glass vase from above the fridge and waving a backward thanks to him, plunked the bouquet in it and kept stirring.

That was it? No welcoming arms wrapped around him? No lingering kisses? Maybe he had made a mistake. Maybe Natalie was not what he'd hoped for. Then, she turned around.

Chapter Seventeen
Cindy
Finding Peace

Cindy stood by the baggage carrousel holding a squirming little Robby against her shoulder. Where was Dad? He had promised to meet her. She saw her suitcases creeping around on the carrousel belt, one with her clothes, one with Robby's essentials, and two empty ones. Those were the ones she would fill with delicacies and needed items from the states to take back to Costa Rica. Maybe she would buy a few beef filets for Rob who craved them. Her friend Laura told her that as long as the stickers on them said Product of USA, they would go through customs. Still, Laura said to watch the customs officials in Costa Rica to be sure they didn't confiscate those precious meats. She would be sure to when she returned.

Finally, she heard a loud chortle. "Didn't know it

would be so hard to park." Her dad paused with glistening eyes. "My precious first grandbaby. Hi, little buddy." He grabbed Robby from Cindy's arms, and to Cindy's relief, he cuddled with his grandpa. It was going to be okay. It was going to be good. She had made the right decision.

Cindy and Robby settled into the guest room in her father's house. She inhaled the lingering lavender scent her mother had used for years as a room spray and as a personal cologne. She had breathed it in on her dad's neck when he was embracing her. On the way home she heard Dad say he went to storage and retrieved the crib Cindy had used as a baby. Cindy knew it wasn't considered safe by today's standards, and if her mother was alive, she would have poo-pooed it, but she clamped her lips tight and hugged him enthusiastically. She would be with Robby the whole time he was in the crib. After all, Cindy had survived the ancient crib, so why couldn't Robby?

She was just getting settled and feeling comfy and relaxed when Rob called. Something was terribly wrong; she could hear it in his voice, even after he said his hello and told her he loved her. Before she even knew the problem, she immediately began worrying about his MS and his commitment to sobriety. Where was her trust?

Rob gulped and explained in an unsteady voice. An unexpected deluge of rain had flooded the basement area of their little home. They'd just started to add a bedroom and bath, somewhere they could accommodate occasional guests, like Dad. Or, Braydon and Noelle. It was planned so anyone who visited could stay with them instead of an expensive hotel. Rob's voice was a bit wobbly. "Brian, the manager, remember him?" he asked. "He helped me, and got some of the landscape workers to help. It took hours of scooping up mud and sweeping wet dirt. A mess, but we saved it." Then he added with a lilt in his voice, "Several AA friends and two from my MS therapy group came by to help. They even brought pizza."

Cindy always worried when he got emotional. Still, she reminded herself, it was part of the deal of being in AA and having a debilitating disease like multiple sclerosis. Rob was a strong man physically, and he had a strong faith. How could her dream man be anything else?

She whispered some of the verses from 1Corinthians 13 under her breath. "Love is patient, love is kind . . . It does not dishonor others, it is not self-seeking, it is not easily angered, it keeps no record of wrongs. It always protects, always trusts, always hopes, always perseveres. Love never fails."

She hung up the landline phone and blew out a sigh of relief. Selfishly, she admitted, she was glad she hadn't been there during the flooding. Those situations often harbored disease born bacteria from stagnant water. Robby could have gotten sick, or she and Rob could have. She hoped he and all the helpers had taken precautions and worn face masks. Praying a thank you praise she joined her dad at the TV. He was watching a stock car race she thought she'd have no interest in. Inspired by his enthusiasm, she got caught up in it. Racing wildly around a track in cool cars sounded like fun. Maybe a release from tension.

Chapter Eighteen
Jaeda
Decision

Connie wiggled her toes under the down comforter. The naps Shane Sullivan had suggested seemed to help her mood and her balance a lot. She felt a lot of movement in her tummy. Even she couldn't get it. Or, wouldn't? Two babies? Was God giving her a message? She had been so excited knowing she was pregnant, but the confirmation had thrown her for a huge loop. Why she had kept it from Jaeda she didn't know. Maybe because it was so scary. Still, he deserved to know and to help deal with this new discovery. Maybe she was too controlling. Yes, that was it. She had become a control freak after her business had blossomed. Yet, she had given a lot of business control to Doreen. Things seemed to be going well in Corona del Mar at Winning Designs.

Feeling more like her old self and not so out of

sorts, she grabbed her cellphone from the bedside table. The least she could do was keep tabs on her design firm. What she got was the option to leave a message. Where was Doreen? It was only 4 p.m. in California. Winning Designs should still be open for business. Hopefully, she was assisting a prominent diva, even a movie star. After an hour, her phone binged chiming "Baby, Baby." By the time she picked it up there was only a message.

~

"Hey, Con! I hope you are feeling better. Melanie told us all about your pg probs. I am so excited for you and Jaeda. Do you know yet if it's two boys, two girls, or a combo? Time to start designing newborn clothes, a biggie in Newport. You could make your million just with those. You'll even have free models. Guess I will be left out of that gig. I love you and am praying."

Connie clicked off her phone. Was that what she was becoming, a new designer for layettes? She shuffled into the crib room, formerly her work room and currently occupied by Vivian. Fortunately, the kind woman was shopping at Kierland tonight, hopefully strolling the sidewalks filled with tourists and enjoying the opulent displays of fancy attire. The crib was folded up and set against a wall. Jaeda had organized everything so Vivian could occupy the room. But, he forgot to hide the yellow fabric still hanging limp on one side of the collapsed crib.

She fondled the fabric printed with stars and bunnies and hearts. It would certainly do for either sex. It was cute and shouted baby, but this was the twenty-first century, and her baby boy or girl, or both, needed to have its own special signature. "I need to know, Lord," she whispered.

Jaeda and Vivian walked into the room in step. Had they practiced that? Connie stuffed a laugh at her silly thought. She turned to them both while supporting her big belly with both hands. She felt a grin overpowering her face. Raising her hands, she announced, "I need to know!"

~

Jaeda and Connie nuzzled each other. She elbowed him pushing him lightly into a seat in the waiting room. When she signed in on the obligatory clipboard, the receptionist cocked her head. "Twins?" she asked with wide smile. Connie nodded. "I think so. Actually, know so. Long story." The young woman with the stud in her nose and the streaks of purple hair nodded. "Doctor will be with you in a few."

Jaeda wasn't totally on board with Dr. H. He knew she was featured in the Top Docs issue of Phoenix Magazine, apparently voted there by her peers. One of the other bank managers had shared that her daughter Alison, a former patient of Dr. H., had twins last year. Alison's twins scared Jaeda. One was born severely disabled; the other boy was almost off the scale brilliant. What had happened? If Dr. H. was so great, couldn't she have prevented that? Or, at least tried?

Connie was led into an examining room, hoisted onto the table and feet placed in the dratted stirrups. Jaeda hated those metal things. Surely there was another more sensitive way to examine a pregnant woman. He sat silently, waiting as usual. Just as the doctor sauntered in and started her exam, another woman in a printed uniform opened the door and touched Dr. H. on the arm. She gestured for the doctor to follow her. Dr. H. nodded and said, "Be back in a moment. Sorry."

Later, Jaeda wondered how sorry she was. Connie laid on the table with feet in cold stirrups for almost a half hour. She was squirming, trying to be brave and patient. Jaeda was squirming, too, but not patient. "This is ridiculous!"

His voice must have carried to the front office. An attendant flew to open the door. Jaeda thought later to feel sorry for the woman, the bearer of bad news. "So sorry," she apologized. "Doctor had an emergency C-section for twins."

"So?" Jaeda couldn't control his mouth. "What kind of doctor would leave a patient for over half an hour in stirrups on the table?" The young woman's face blanked, and apologetic words stumbled out. "Get up, Connie. Get dressed. We are out of here."

~

He remembered a bank client telling him about a wonderful doctor who only attended to women expecting multiple deliveries. What was that woman's name? Searching his data base, he brought up several. Harriett, Rose, Jennifer, Jean. He would have to go against bank policy to contact each, but Connie and his babies were more important.

After several furtive phone calls, he hit pay dirt. Harriett remembered because her niece had had twins. "This doctor is amazing, Mr. Wayman. She monitors every nuance of the pregnancy. She is actually internationally renowned. Please call her."

Jaeda took down the number after thanking Harriett and dialed.

Fortunately, he remembered Harriett's niece's name and blatantly used it as a reference. In two days they would see Dr. Francois.

"Oh, my gosh, oh, my gosh!" Jaeda was practically dancing, bringing back memories of his first dance with Connie at the Newport Pavilion. He wanted to reproduce it, so he took her hand and started shuffling sideways humming a tune. Connie laughed, for the first time in a long time, melodically. He wrapped his arms around her and nuzzled her neck. "It's going to be all right, Con. It's going to be okay." Her full mouth puckered. The kiss was one of the sexiest they'd ever had.

~

Vivian noticed the difference. Connie and Jaeda were lovers again. She sighed and raised her hands to God in the privacy of her temporary room. She immediately began to pull clothes out of the drawers and pack her suitcase. She was no longer needed here. It saddened her a bit, but it filled her heart with joy, too. She heard from her Bill he was feeling much better, even accepted a houseguest, Natalie's new friend, boyfriend, whomever. He sounded nice, and Nat really needed someone to pay special attention to her, maybe even fall in love with her.

Then, because worry was part of her makeup as a mom, she wondered about Melanie. Those two girls needed closure, the closure of love.

Chapter Nineteen
Natalie
Discoveries

Larry let out a low whistle, then an earth-shattering hoot, the kind his dad taught him when he was twelve. They had been playing pickup basketball down the block in the vacant lot, just them. It was Larry's birthday and a rare occasion for Da to spend time with him. He hadn't missed having a party or a fancy cake. When he made a difficult free throw, standing amazed looking at the torn basket of the old dirt court, Da ran up and high-fived him, a face-splitting grin taking over his brown cheeks. Then, he put two fingers in his mouth and said, "Do this, boy. Try it. I know you have the gift." Larry did, and the whistle he'd later call a wolf whistle erupted loudly. Da grinned again, and this time he hugged him. Larry would never forget that hug. It was the best birthday present ever. He squeezed his eyes shutting out the memory and gazed at Natalie.

Who was this woman? Not sweet-faced Natalie with the sprinkling of freckles and bouncy long hair. What had she done? Why the transformation?

Natalie grinned widely, this time showing teeth so white they were almost blinding. "You like?"

When Larry stood speechless with mouth gaping, she asked, "No? Too much?"

He finally found his voice, and his words croaked out from a nodding head. He felt like a bobble head. "Yes," he repeated "Yes," after clearing his throat. "I don't understand." He waited for a response, but got none. "You trying out for a play? Or a movie part?"

Nat giggled that delightful sound he liked. "No, nothing that dramatic. Just decided to do a makeover. For fun, and for myself, my self-esteem." Her new eyebrows raised up in question.

She almost forgot about the eggs. When she started to serve them, she gestured for him to take a seat at the kitchen counter. His legs were so long she noticed that even with the high stool his feet sat firmly on the floor. Bryce's didn't reach, but Billy's did, barely.

Larry started to dig in until he heard Nat's clear voice praying. He put his fork down and clasped the two hands reaching across the counter at him. When was he supposed to open his eyes? Oh, when she said "Amen" and squeezed his hands.

"So, what do you think? Really." Nat's face was a puzzle, a beautiful puzzle, a new face.

Larry put a hand over his mouth to cough. "Sorry. Just so shocked and taken back by the new you." Were her eyes starting to mist? He reached across the Formica again and touched her fingers. "I suppose this is a stupid guy thing to say, but I hope you didn't do it for me." He grasped one of her hands. "I really loved the way you looked when we first met."

"You did?"

"Yes. You looked so natural, so happy in your own skin." He felt his ears burning. "Do you understand? It was so refreshing to meet someone like you."

He shoved a big bite of eggs in his mouth and took a long drink of the coffee. He felt he needed to justify his comments. "You didn't put on any airs, you didn't try to impress me. I just loved the real you."

Had he just used the word love? Twice? Natalie was confused. Maybe it was a flip comment.

"Yes, Larry, I did it partly for you. But I did it mostly for myself, something I'd wanted to do for a long time. Meeting you gave me the courage." She crumbled her napkin and scooped up the plates. Dumping them in the sink to rinse later, she spun around. "Did you decide what you'd like to do here in Newport?"

Larry nodded. She prayed he wouldn't pick up and leave.

"I don't know much about Newport, but you did give some fun ideas." He followed her to the sink and wrapped his arms around her. "I think the boat ride would be fun. I've always been curious about movie stars' homes. Can we do that today?" Then, he added, "I'd love to do a pickup basketball game in

Venice Beach in late afternoon. You want to come?" Seeing the cloud of puzzlement in her face, he said, "You don't have to. It's fun. Only guys, though."

~

They stood in line to board the Grey Goose. Most of the people towed young kids behind them. So young, Nat reflected, they would have no concept of the stars' homes or who the stars had been. Still, just being on a boat and cruising would probably thrill them. She and Larry found seats up front. At least they had a good view. Nat had been on a harbor excursion several times with out of town visitors, but never on the birthday one in honor of The Duke. It was special, so she gave it a lot of attention trying to ignore the tantalizing male aroma of the man next to her. What was that scent? Aftershave or cologne? Or, just male? She looked up at his moustache and sparse, but obviously deliberate, chin hair on his handsome face and wondered. Was he here just because she had invited him, or because he wanted to be?

After the boat ride, after ogling over the houses of George Burns and Gracie Allen, Nic Cage, Roy Rogers, and Joey Bishop, Larry suggested the bumper cars. Always a bit uncomfortable with so little control, she sucked it up and did it. When he asked about the Ferris wheel, she almost collapsed. Folding her into his arms, he held her closely.

"Not your thing?" She nodded. "Fear of heights?" She nodded again and sunk her face into his chest. He held her, pulling her body against his with her hands gripping the collar of his shirt. "It's okay. We won't do it. Let's go to Venice Beach and play ball."

She would just be a spectator. She would try to be interested. She climbed into her little car with Larry beside her. He gave directions. She complied. Maybe he came here often, not just a weekend to see her. Surely, he must, if he suggested it. Why hadn't he said? Why hadn't she known? Another Larry mystery.

Several years ago she had bought a high-end camera. She'd always loved to take photos, mostly of sunsets and birds. She decided to bring it along to the pick-up game. Maybe she would find a new hobby. She tucked it into her overstuffed car trunk with donations for Goodwill. She felt like donating herself. Would she get a receipt?

Chapter Twenty
Natalie
Disappointment

"Who is this woman?" Melanie held Natalie as far away as possible with her hands gripping Nat's shoulders. She locked eyes with her friend and shook her head vigorously, like she was shaking out demons. Like Lola shook after a bath. "Is this someone I know?" Her loud laugh turned Natalie's face ashen. She hugged Nat and whispered in her ear. "Sorry, girl. Didn't mean to scare you. I love it!" She reached for a tissue and dabbed Nat's eyes. "The New You!"

She led Nat to the faded yard sale sofa in her meager apartment, pushed her down, then sat beside her. Questions burst from her mouth like rapid gunfire.

"Larry?" was the first one. "Bryce? Billy? Someone new?"

"No." Natalie shook her head. "Actually, it was Claire."

Melanie's eyes formed questions. "Claire? Nick's mom? The surfer dude who got married to Emily?"

"She is such an encourager. Gave me gift cards to Stevens and Cross for a makeup redo, one for Robert the fantastic hair stylist at Salon Gregories, a mani-pedi at this cute little place in Corona del Mar where I also got a marvelous neck massage from Lisa. I almost fell asleep, both during the pedicure and the massage. It was such a treat. A treat for myself. One I've needed a long time.

"Oh, Claire also bought a new guest chair for my office. Wait 'til you see it and sit in it."

She bunched up a throw pillow on the sofa, the one that said, "Love is a dog." Melanie had a set of three. The other two said, "My dog's the boss," and "Every day is a dog day." Hugging the first one against her chest, she started to weep, quietly rocking. The sobs suddenly came in ocean waves, racking her body. Melanie held her until the shivering stopped and gently pushed her down on the beat-up sofa and slipped a dog pillow under her new bobbed tresses.

She tucked Nat in, tossing a patchwork quilt her mom had made over her exhausted frame. Lola jumped right up to snuggle against her legs. At first Mel was offended at the canine display of affection to someone other than her, but she was glad Lola was such a sympathetic dog. Mel was worried about Nat. Over the last year they had become best friends, confidants sharing many secrets and worries. Mel worried about Nat's need to find a love, a husband.

They were both almost only twenty-nine, not all that old for their generation. Was it called "X"? Melanie longed, too, for a love, a family and a man who adored her, and kids. Yet, she did have Lola to cuddle with at night. So, she had something.

~

"Coffee's on. Stir your stumps." Melanie's voice caused havoc in Natalie's ears. Where was she? Confused, she sat up and pushed a heavy quilt off. She noticed the pattern. Little log cabins mostly. Very homey, comforting. She needed comforting. She had put herself out to do a total remake. That should have done it. She should feel glamorous, new, in control. Why didn't she? Why didn't she feel glamorous? Had Larry really noticed, really cared? She couldn't remember him complimenting her on the new look, only the old one. Suddenly, Lola jumped up and licked her chin. Ugh! She knew it was a loving gesture. Could a dog's love fulfill the need she so craved?

Melanie placed a cup of aromatic coffee on the side table. What was the wonderful smell? Cinnamon? Hazelnut? Maybe both. She took a sip and coughed. "Sorry. Hot."

Somehow, Nat knew the questions wouldn't stop. Mel was curious, wanted to help, loved her, but had that need to know personality. Melanie was a fixer, maybe the only one of the Candy Canes. Nat braced herself for the onslaught.

"Okay, girl. Time to share. In depth." She smiled encouragingly at Nat and gave her a kiss on the still wet cheek. "What happened? From the beginning. Start with the makeover."

Nat sat up cross-legged and pulled the comforting quilt under her chin. "He . . . he noticed, but said he loved the way I looked before. Fresh-faced, not putting on airs." She clutched the corner of the quilt and sighed. "It was a back-handed compliment. I'm not sure about him, not at all."

"Why? I thought you liked him a lot. Really cool guy you said."

"Thought he was. He is, but so different. I don't mean his race." Nat screwed up her face as if memories were taking over. She lowered her lids. Almost whispering, she lifted her look to Melanie. "Remember when I said Bryce turned me off because of his new look, his ponytail?" Mel nodded.

"Well," she paused, and her face blossomed pink. "Ponytails can be cut."

"Where is this going, Nat?"

"Tattoos."

"What? You saw one?"

Nat choked, almost spitting out her coffee. "Not one. Many."

"How? You weren't intimate, were you?" The question hung in the air like a balloon ready to burst. It wasn't a party balloon with happy sayings on it.

"*No!* He wanted to do this pickup basketball game at Venice Beach. So, I drove him, since we can't both fit on that weird cycle he has. I didn't pay much attention when he got in the car, but when he got out, took off his shirt and yelled to the guys on the beach, I saw. More than I wanted to."

"Explain. In detail." Was Mel repeating herself? Maybe, but . . .

"I stopped counting."

When Mel said, "Go ahead," she did.

"Maybe six, or seven," she corrected herself. "Big one on his back; one on each arm and each leg, one on chest. I think I lost count."

"I have no major problem with tattoos, even dated a guy who had one. Still, this sounds extreme."

"Yeh. Threw me for a loop."

"I know Pastor Terry and some of the other Hillsong pastors in Scottsdale have tattoos." She paused. "Not that many, and not all over their bodies. Mostly hidden by clothes, some even explained in their messages. Who knows, maybe Kenton at our Mariners Church in Irvine has some hidden ones. However, I doubt if Laurie would accept that." She snickered and locked eyes with Natalie, then squeezed her hands. "Tell me about them. Why did you see them?"

"He had changed into beach basketball attire in my bathroom. Well, actually stripped into shorts under his long pants, and a sleeveless tee. Both of which he took off to play. At first, I saw the ones on his upper arms. I decided to act nonchalant, not be judgmental. When he removed the running pants and the tee, it unnerved me. Hadn't expected it, and he hadn't warned me. It was like there was no longer Larry, just tattoos to define him. Why did he get them? Where? Who, what man, can I trust?"

Melanie squeezed her hands harder. After letting go, she must have had a flash thought. "Have you reconnected with Billy? Candy's brother?"

Natalie shook her head. "Not since the aborted Ferris wheel incident. Why? You think I should?"

~

Natalie prayed. She screwed up so much courage she hardly knew herself. When she dialed, she prayed again. Larry had left last night to go back to Arizona, and she felt a huge relief. He was a really nice guy. Handsome and courteous, but the chemistry just wasn't right. And the tattoos had set her off. She remembered her friend Jean's son who had gotten many, too many, while in prison. Is that where, and why, Larry had them? Naw, not Larry.

She reminded herself, Billy was cute and had been attentive, even traveling to Scottsdale to woo her when she visited the Waymans. Besides, he was Candy's brother. She had known Billy for umpteen years, remembered him screaming encouraging yells when the Candy Canes were swimming final laps for the winning championships. He was a right-on guy. A guy she could trust. He had tried to pursue a relationship with her, but she put him off after he'd scared her atop a Ferris wheel. Maybe he wasn't the clingy type. Maybe she should give him another chance. The thought of possibly being Candy's sister-in-law exhilarated her. That would be so special. *Here I go jumping the gun again.*

She fluffed up her hair, her new bob, and dialed. Stupid gesture when Billy couldn't even see her, and she avoided Facetime, except when she and Larry had used it during when he had been following Bryce. Too intimate. He could have seen every pore on her face and the zit on her chin. No, no – not her style, certainly not her comfort level. She was so surprised when Billy picked up she fell back on the faded fabric of Mel's sofa.

"Well, hi, after all this time." His voice sounded

happy to hear from her. Hopefully, he didn't think this was a desperate call. She found her own voice with a lot of help from God and Melanie's prayers.

"Yes, it's me. The girl afraid of heights. I am trying to get over that." She took a very deep breath. "Would you be willing to try again with me?"

"What? Ferris wheel? Mmm, maybe. You wanna go tonight?"

She hadn't thought of that. Tonight? Now? So soon? Could she do it?

"Uh, maybe. *You* free tonight?" She hoped he was teasing, maybe really had a big deal brewing to sell a one hundred-thousand-dollar car for his resale dealership. He sounded so upbeat, even offered to pick her up in an hour. Could she get ready? Reproduce the wonderful makeup, look like her new you?

Billy pulled up, actually revved up, in a red Maserati. Probably another one of his "borrowed" cars, from a client who'd said to drive it around town and get people curious. Was she, Natalie, part of the deal? Was Billy using her and their "sort of" date as a marketing ploy?

Chapter Twenty-one
Vivian
A Lesson

Vivian scooted into the driveway and parked her little cycle. Bill could deal with it later, parking it in the huge garage. If she could, she would have slapped herself on the back for riding it to and from the airport. She hoped Bill would be proud of her.

"What in Sam Hill were you doing riding that little cycle? Were you crazy?"

"Nice to see you, too." Vivian clenched her fists and glared at her husband. "Seems like you are feeling better." She knew her eyes had fireworks flares in them, but she didn't care.

"You abandoned me, took off on some no-nonsense fling."

Vivian set down her duffle, and stomped out of the room to make a pot of coffee. Mr. "Master Bill" stood staring. She was sure her slightly plump, petite frame filled his eyes. She hoped he got the message.

Bill ruminated. He fiddled with the napkin on the counter, folded it and refolded. What had happened to him in the past year since he and Vivian had married? He knew he had been so in love with her, but he hadn't measured up, even to himself. Maybe flowers? A special night out? He needed to call Bill, Jr. He loved his stepmom Vivian; he was young and gifted in romance. He could help.

Slinking into his den, he dialed.

~

"What, Dad? You aren't serious?"

Bill, Sr. tugged at his ear. An old habit he thought he'd abandoned. Apparently not. He pulled on the lobe and let it all out to his son. "She walked out on me, twice. Once to go to Scottsdale to help Connie when Jaeda called sounding stressed, but she hadn't been asked; and now when she came home." He sighed dramatically. "She's in our bedroom now. Alone. Drinking coffee. Flavored."

Big Bill held the phone from his ear. Why was his son laughing? What happened to respecting your parents?

"Dad, have you heard of mutual agreement?"

"What do you mean? Your mom always respected my wishes."

"Yeh, Dad. That was a zillion years ago. This is the twenty-first century, and Vivian is a modern woman." Bill, Jr. paused and took a long breath. "Dad, she loves you. You gotta learn to go with the flow. Be more understanding, more empathetic. Be . . . more modern. Weren't you the one, the loving husband, the groom, who bought her the little cycle?

Didn't you encourage her to ride it?"

Big Bill put the phone down and leaned his chin in his hands. He guessed he had a lot to learn.

Chapter Twenty-two
Jaeda
Choices

Jaeda was happy. Vivian and Sandra had finally left. He had Connie all to his own. She seemed more secure now that she had confessed leaving him out of the loop about bearing twins. He decided to not go there. No questions. Just trust, and holding her close in his arms. He felt her body melt into his and smelled the enticing scent she wore. She had never told him what it was. He needed to ask and find it so he could order a huge bottle on the internet. Maybe if he looked on the bathroom counter? *Duh. I hope I'm not one of those clueless husbands. I guess I was, sort of, when her belly got so huge.*

Connie stirred in his embrace. He curled his arms around her tightly, and she snuggled in. He was surprised at her question. "What, Jaede, do you think about my starting a designer line of baby clothes?"

He pulled back from her and searched her face. Her eyebrows formed feathery questions, and her sparkling eyes almost glittered. Was the real Connie returning?

He ignored her question as she fell asleep and hugged her closer, nuzzling his mouth in her ivory neck.

~

The call from Doreen made Connie tremble. She almost put the phone down from her shaking hand.

"Cons, you won't believe this." Doreen used her nickname, then excitedly prattled on. "I just took twenty orders for the layette today, for babies that haven't even been born yet.

At almost a thousand dollars each!" Doreen's voice shook. Was she as excited as Doreen? Or, was Doreen afraid Connie couldn't produce them fast enough?

Connie sat in the ugly recliner, the one she tried to convince Jaeda not to buy, the one he said reminded him of his father's favorite perch, and he wanted one, too. At least, because of her designer influence, it wasn't an ugly brown. Instead, it was an ugly red. Matched the sofas, sort of. She ran her fingers along the arms not yet worn badly by too many bodies sitting in it. Had to admit the comfort of it felt good on her back, and the babies in her belly rested. When he came home from the bank she would tell him about the baby designs. She knew he would be thrilled.

~

"Baby stuff? You're an international designer now. Isn't this a peg below?"

Connie wanted to slap him in the worst way. Yes, Winning Designs was his endeavor, too, but she was the designer, the one who created. The mysterious entrepreneur group had backed it with cash; and, after his calculation mistake, he had modeled to make up for his error. All the group asked was for her to pass it on. Other than tithing at church, she hadn't figured out where. It would come in time.

"Why aren't you happy? This is a new avenue for Winning Designs and us. We could make thousands just from baby stuff. In fact," she paused, "I could design mother and daughter and mother and boy baby outfits, too."

She grabbed his face and pulled it toward her. "What is wrong with that?"

"Do I have to model as the father to be?"

Connie chortled, and four legs and four arms punched her from the inside. "You are a trip, Mr. Wayman! However, you do have a great idea." She sniggered with a hand over her lips. Jaeda looked stricken. His eyes were propped open with toothpicks. She grinned and nodded and winked. She loved teasing him. Or, was she?

Chapter Twenty-three
Natalie and Melanie
Hospital Visit

Natalie swatted the air and slapped at her face. How did a mosquito get in? She hated the little buggers. Never could figure out why God made them, ants and those dirty pigeons. She added spiders to that list, too. The buzzing sound stopped for a moment. Did she get him? Naw, it started again. She tossed the covers off, wiggled upright and tugged off the pink sleeping mask mussing her new hairdo. Then, she noticed her phone jumping around on the nightstand. Who? At 3 a.m. Might as well answer. Might be an emergency. It was.

The distant, professional voice asked, "Is this Natalie Newcomer?" She nodded and realized the caller couldn't see her. "Yes," she finally whispered hoping it wasn't a robo call to sell her something. In the middle of the night? Even those idiots didn't call then. Clutching the sheet, she started to shake when she heard the woman's next words.

~

Melanie knew something was wrong with Nat. Nat never called after ten, except once recently around midnight when she was stressed about the Bryce, Billy, and now Larry, triangle. She looked at the digital clock's orange numbers. 3:30! Good thing she was a light sleeper. Lola was snuggled against her left leg dreaming. At least Mel assumed from the snorts and body jerks.

Briefly, she wondered if she did those, too. Yikes, she hoped not, if she was ever blessed to have a husband lying next to her. Pushing her bangs out of her eyes, she picked up her phone.

"I'll be right there. Hang, girl, hang on."

~

"I don't know why they called me." She wiped her eyes with the back of her hand. "Yes, I guess I do. The woman explained. Other than his own I.D., she only found a few business cards. One was mine, and it was the only local one. Also, he had moaned my name." Natalie wrung her hands while Melanie drove to Hoag Hospital. Thank goodness it was close for both of them, just off Pacific Coast Highway. Melanie started to tremble. Her mind went back several years ago to when she had caused Doreen's accident and they had all gathered at Hoag with Braydon Lovejoy leading them in prayer. She thought of the old quip "What goes around, comes around." This time it was Larry.

A nurse led them to the ICU unit while explaining he was in a lot of pain and they couldn't stay long.

Nat asked about broken bones. "No," the woman smiled. "Just royally banged up. Badly. Fortunately, no surgery needed, at least not yet." She turned to both women before opening the door to the room. "Not sure how you got in. Maybe because he has no relatives and you are close?" She seemed to zero in on Natalie. "He needs someone. I hope you are that someone." Nat squirmed. Was she?

The nurse finally pushed open the door, then turned again. "He's only in ICU," she said, almost as an apology, "because he is so badly bruised all over, and we had room tonight."

Larry stirred. He was semi-awake. Nat wasn't sure if that was good, or scary. She found the courage to take his hand, a hand that was bandaged with only finger tips poking through. She gently squeezed those tips, and he smiled. Well, weakly. "Can you talk, Larry? What happened?"

She wasn't sure if she should ask, but her propensity to know took over. Why was she here and not someone from his family? Then, she remembered him off-handedly saying he really had no family. Sadness engulfed her, and she touched his fingertips again.

"Hi, Nat." He smiled weakly through the gauze wrapping his face. "Tank you fur coming. Donna know wha I do without you." His words were slurred. Probably from medications. He must be in a lot of pain. What was she to do? How should she respond? She really liked Larry, a lot. But, she wasn't in love with him.

Nat believed deeply in friendship. She swore to never abandon a friend. That was part of the Candy

Cane vow. She clung to it now. Larry was a friend, a dear friend, who treated her like gold, even came to California to spend time with her twice. Not to mention all the time he'd spent tracking down Bryce who really had abandoned her after the aborted sky diving jump.

She touched his face at the small opening on his cheek that was not covered by bandages. His eyes flickered. "That was s-sho nice." She felt like a fool. That one touch seemed to make such a difference. Thank you, God.

Suddenly, he noticed Melanie standing quietly behind her. "Who zat person? Ove zere?" He forced the slurred words out, then raised one bandaged hand and pointed feebly.

Melanie stepped forward and smiled. It must have been her most engaging smile because Natalie swore the bandages on Larry's face almost fell off.

~

What had happened there? Nat was still trying to figure it out. Larry had been so grateful to see her, and she was glad she had come. Yet, when he saw Melanie, it was like a burst of fire. Something had exploded. Stars seemed to hover over his hospital bed and burst from Melanie's eyes.

"I don't know," Mel said, but her voice shook a little. "Nice guy. That's all." Natalie detected a smirk from her vantage on the passenger seat. What really had happened there?

Chapter Twenty-four
Connie and Jaeda
Pinning, and Modeling?

Connie sat at her drawing board and squirmed trying to get closer. She tried raising the board above her belly, then lowering it way down. Nothing quite worked. Finally, she tilted it more. She grabbed a marking pen, not her usual design pen, but it functioned. She tried to design mother/daughter outfits, but nothing came. When the idea in her head finally germinated, she laughed. Would Jaeda even accept it? Or, would he be offended? She would need him again to model. Who would be Baby?

She missed her pinner, cutter, dressmaker in California. Alice had been so fun, yet professional. Even Jaeda had gotten along famously with her when he had been pressed into modeling. They quipped back and forth bringing levity to the designing process. The dogs liked her, too. Little

Jake quivered all over every time she entered the fitting room, and Candy's big lout Striker wagged his rump furiously while drooling. Thank goodness Doreen knew how to calm the large, borrowed dog. It had been a lightning bolt of brilliance on Doreen's part, the idea to incorporate dogs and matching dog and owner outfits in Connie's plaid line, and borrow Candy's obedient, complacent old dog. Doreen had intuitive marketing strategy, cared so much for the business and loved her role in it – the modeling, speaking engagements, photo shoots. Even with her gimp leg. Before she and Jaeda had moved to Scottsdale, Connie spent several sleepless nights and worried days debating if she should ask Doreen to take over the Corona del Mar boutique in California. Could she run it and still model on L.A. fashion ramps? Finally, she and Jaeda sat down with her and presented a plan. Doreen was ecstatic, had always wanted to be part of something special in fashion retail. Hands were clasped, papers were signed, and Doreen became the manager and one-fourth owner of Winning Designs. As well as its only model, until the baby designs.

Sandy, her personal seamstress in Scottsdale, and now new pinner, knocked on her door. She was a little startled, then remembered she'd told Clarence at the guard gate to just let her in. She liked him, but where was Larry? He had been gone for almost two weeks. Sandy wrapped her arms around Connie, as much as she could with Connie's bulk. They both snickered as Sandy gently patted her belly.

"Yikes, girl! You could burst any sec."

"Not due for five more weeks." Sandy rolled her

expressive green eyes, raised her brown eyebrows and did a silent whistle with pursed lips. "Okay. Let's roll. What do you have for me?"

They worked together almost as well as she and Alice had. Even little Jake took to Sandy. Must have been her smell. She had three dogs of her own, all rescues like Jake. Sandy's mouth was full of straight pins, but she tried to mumble through the metal. "You sure you want this hemline so long? Maybe in the baby's dress, but the mom's should be shorter. Don't you think? And more flaring, softer?"

Connie nodded and kept sweeping her pen across the big paper on her drawing board. This was going to be perfect. She was so glad Sandy felt comfortable making suggestions with another pair of eyes. She showed Sandy the results. Sandy hooted – something Alice would never have done. It was a fun affirmation. Sandy kept pinning the soft pink material on the mannequin, made some adjustments and stood back. They both admired the mom dress and the matching baby princess dress. "This will be a big seller," Sandy said. Connie noticed her eyes misted a bit. What had she missed about Sandy? Then, she remembered Sandy had only boys.

Jaeda whistled a lullaby as he slammed the door. He was out of tune and knew it. The melody clung to his heart and in his brain. Soon, he would insist on another ultrasound. He wanted to know . . . girls, or boys, or both. He stopped when he heard two female voices laughing. How nice for Connie to have a friend over. Until, said friend whooped, "He's here! Now, we can work on the father and son outfits." He almost spun around and walked out. He would have if Jake hadn't given him away with a woof and leaping at his legs. Little traitor.

Chapter Twenty-five
Melanie
Sparks

Natalie and Melanie went back the next day to visit Larry. He was sitting up in bed watching a TV show and yelling, "Door One, idiot." He smiled at Nat, clicked off the TV with the corded remote in his hand, and squeezed her fingertips with his. Then, he noticed Melanie standing off to the side. The air became electrified again, Natalie was sure. She felt the sparks. The hair stood up on her arms, like when she was tugging the sheets off her bed for the laundry and her fingers got zapped by the static electricity in the dry air.

"Uh, gonna get some coffee. Anyone want?" No one paid attention to her.

She stirred a massive amount of creamer in the dark brew, sat at a long cafeteria table and reflected. She was worried about Mel and Larry, but God's

Word said to not worry about each day, that tomorrow would have worries of its own. Or, something like that. Why hadn't she memorized Bible verses as a kid? Or, even as an adult? She had known she could look them up from the Concordance in the pink Bible her mom had given her as a teen. Now, in church, and during her morning devotions, she used the Bible ap on her cell phone. Did that count?

She finally went back up to Larry's room holding her coffee cup tight, like it might disappear.

"What is going on here?" Nat bit her lip so hard she felt the taste of blood.

Two bodies raised like apparitions from the hospital bed, one half-sitting and struggling to pull a sheet up with bandaged hands, the other leaping to the linoleum floor. Melanie stood utterly still clasping her hands in front of her blue patterned skirt. Larry tucked his one bound hand beneath the white hospital sheets. The other one rested on top of the sheet, bruised. Nat noticed an unusual bruise on his wrist. Heart-shaped. How odd. Was it a God sign?

His eyes looked strange. Embarrassed? Sad? Confused? Yes, Nat decided, confused. She wiped her hand across her lip and tasted blood again. Melanie and Larry? What kind of situation was she in the middle of? What did the heart-shaped bruise on his arm mean? Maybe nothing she decided. Just a fluke.

Natalie tightened both hands around the styro cup. "I'm going for … more coffee."

Larry's eyes glazed over. "Wait, Natalie, please."

She spun around. "Mel, would you mind giving Natalie and me a minute alone?"

Mel? Not even Melanie? Mel? Natalie thought she was going to be sick. Good thing she was in a hospital.

~

Melanie, usually a chatterbox, was silent on the way home. Natalie was glad, because she had nothing to say to Melanie. Finally, Melanie cleared her throat. "Sorry 'bout that." Nat just nodded, wasn't even sure Mel could see her in the dark shadows of the car. She didn't care. She didn't even understand why she felt angry, but fury bubbled up from her heart to her throat and her swollen lip. She dabbed her lip with a tissue and it showed pink; not lipstick pink, but the fading color of drying blood. It was her own stupid fault biting her lip. Finally, she found her croaky voice.

"It's not my call who cares for whom." Gosh, Noelle's English teachering must have rubbed off on her. *Whom*? She waited for a response from Melanie, but after a long silence, she just shifted closer to the passenger door and pressed her nose to the cold window. Mel finally pulled up to Nat's condo and put the car in park.

"Maybe talk to you later. K?"

"Sure. Thanks for the ride."

~

Natalie wasn't sure what had happened there in the hospital room, and the car. She and Melanie had become so close, really like true sisters. She started to kneel by her bed to pray, not something she did often because of her back pain from the bad sky diving incident when Bryce left her prone on the hard ground. Shoving her fist into the most painful spot on her lower back, she bent her knees and grabbed the edge of her bedspread. She prayed. Again, she wished she had memorized verses. As she petitioned God, an idea came through. She reached for the old pink Bible and looked up the word forgiveness. Turning to the New Testament, she found what she wanted in Mark 11:25. **"And when you stand praying, if you hold anything against anyone, forgive them, so that your Father in heaven may forgive you your sins."**

She struggled to stand, wobbling on her legs. Picking up her phone she hesitated, then dialed.

~

Natalie and Melanie slipped quietly into Larry's hospital room. Day three. Nat felt like a second string, maybe a third. She was trying to figure out what had happened between her friends, when Larry cried out. "I can't walk!" He was sitting with his feet hanging over the side of the bed swinging his legs. One foot hung down, and its ankle was taped. His face twisted in confusion. One hand clasped his ankle. It had a heart-shaped red bruise on it.

Mel rushed to grip his hand and squeezed it tenderly, at least from Nat's perspective. Electricity, again. The air sparked. Nat felt it again on her arms, even the back of her neck.

"I can't move my foot. I can't put any pressure on it. I need to get back to my job." His shaky voice cracked.

Nat pulled at the sheets wrapped around his legs and felt his ankle. She swallowed a "damn." It did look and feel weak, maybe broken, or at least traumatized. She rang for the nurse. When the woman in the blouse printed with yellow happy faces rushed in, she looked at Larry's swollen ankle and said in a no-nonsense voice, "X-ray."

Chapter Twenty-six
Connie
Plaid, PT, Patients

"You look adorable, Jaeda." Maybe that wasn't the right comment from Sandy. "Actually, you are a hunk." Whew, Sandy had redeemed herself, and hopefully Jaeda. Didn't matter to little Jake; he must have remembered the design times a few years ago when he got to snuggle in Jaeda's arm in a cute plaid outfit. Loyal as they were, dogs could also be fickle.

Jaeda sighed, loudly. He struggled to not move on the platform while Sandy pinned. He knew it would be faster if he stood still. "Stop wiggling, Mister," she blew the words out from a mouth full of metal. "Now, doggie here is the perfect model. Not even a twitch."

Jaeda almost choked. Jake was perfect, and he wasn't? What was this world coming to? His world?

~

Connie gave a thumb up and hugged goodbye to Sandy. It had been a good session, but she was tired. Babies were doing gymnastics big time. She hefted her belly with both palms and started to slide off the stool, but her dangling legs didn't cooperate. She stretched out her legs so her toes would touch the carpet and balance her. Instead, the stool scooted backward on its own path; her ankle, caught in one of the stool's legs, twisted, and she slammed onto the floor on her backside. So much for her plan to check the crockpot dinner. She was trying to be a good wife, not a perfect one, but at least good. The crockpot sizzled. After lifting Connie up, Jaeda ran to pull the plug.

"Why, Jaede, why?" Connie sobbed in his arms as he embraced her bulky body. Her tears rained like an April downpour on his starched shirt. "I'm so clumsy, so stupid."

"You are neither, Cons, you are big time pregnant." His voice sounded angry. He announced a decision. "It's time to see that other doctor, the one who specializes in multiple births."

~

Connie stumbled into Spine Scottsdale leaning heavily on Jaeda. The new baby doctor, Carrie Francois, had written another prescription for physical therapy. She was game. It had felt so good the other time with the heat pads and those T.E.M.S. electrical things that stimulated her muscles. Because of her pregnancy, they couldn't be put on her back, just her leg. Nevertheless, the massage therapy felt so good, and the ice after was soothing.

She turned her head toward the large man on the

therapy table next to her. Crutches were propped next to it. What was Larry doing there? Larry, their favorite gate guard in their community. She couldn't help but notice he looked kind of beat up, and forlorn. Jaeda had walked back to the table with her to settle her in.

"Larry? That you? Our Larry?"

The lightly bearded brown face turned toward them. Was the expression on it embarrassment or pain? Jaeda held out his hand. "Hey, man. You okay?" Then, he laughed softly. "Stupid question. Why are you here? Or, as my mom would say, is it none of my beeswax?"

Connie almost choked on the old expression coming from her husband. Jaeda was, after all, pretty traditional. She reminded herself she felt blessed with that. She twisted as best she could and reached out her hand across the empty space between the two physical therapy tables. Her fingertips touched Larry's as she said a prayer. Then, her womanly curiosity took over.

"Larry, what happened?"

Before he could answer, Shane Sullivan swooped over with those clear plastic medical gloves on, told Larry to rest his right leg on a pillow and started to massage his left foot and ankle. Larry winced, then turned toward Jaeda.

"Could have been worse. Could have been beaten up. Guess I was lucky."

"No, Larry," Connie said, "you were blessed. Protected."

"Yeh, by whom?"

Chapter Twenty-seven
Melanie
Sharing

Melanie was still stunned about what had happened between them in the hospital. Whatever it was, Larry was gone, back in Scottsdale where his job was. This time he flew since his little cycle was totally wrecked. Fortunately, he had good accident insurance, but he was very frustrated those teen boys got away with damaging his cycle, and him. Logan Lovejoy had called the police who called the paramedics and transported him to the hospital. Logan had also contacted Allstate Insurance and waited with the cycle until one of its adjusters arrived. Next, he called Natalie, but she had already received a call from Hoag Hospital. Melanie knew one of God's angels on earth had rescued Larry.

She still felt his touch, still felt a connection. She knew he wasn't a believer, but maybe . . . someday.

She remembered discussing his over the top tattoos with Natalie. How Nat couldn't deal with them, and how Melanie had no problem. Did she still feel that way? She wasn't sure, but she knew she wanted to be with Larry.

"Melanie?" Connie pulled the door open. Why hadn't the guard rung her to tell her she had a visitor? Oh, probably Mel was on the okay list. "Hi, friend. Why are you here?" She felt embarrassed even asking that. Did it really matter? Friends were welcome any time. Connie opened her arms and embraced her Candy Cane sister around her big belly. Big hugs, no reservations. Thank goodness the guest room was up to speed.

"What about your job, Mel? Your dog?" Connie hoped Melanie hadn't blown her job, and being the dog lover she was, she worried about the one Mel had adopted.

"It's summer break, and I didn't sign up for teaching at any day camps. Lola is with Natalie who reluctantly agreed to take care of her."

"You could have brought her here," Connie said. "Jake would have loved the companionship. Anyway, what made you decide to come to Arizona?" She still didn't want Melanie to feel unwelcome, but it was so sudden, and she was curious.

"I don't know why I'm here. Well, I sort of do." Melanie swiped a cheek. Was she crying?

Connie didn't understand. "Catch me up, Mel. This pregnancy has flown me for a loop."

"I can't understand it myself, but I really care for

117

him. I felt zingers in my chest when I walked into his hospital room."

"Hospital room?" Connie was confused. Why hadn't she known about all this?

Melanie finally exploded. She shared the almost romance situation, as she called it, between Natalie and Larry. Then, the feeling she had when she first met him in the hospital. She knew from Natalie that he was a big man with a bold presence, but under the sheets, he looked so vulnerable. To Melanie, his dark eyes screamed "help me."

"That's why you are here, why you need to be here," Connie said. "Follow your heart, Mel, just like I did with Jaeda."

Connie tucked Melanie in the queen size bed and pulled a fuzzy blanket over her to ward off the AC that they always had on in Arizona to combat the intense heat. Tomorrow they would go together to find Larry. Since he had taken off a few weeks from his position as security guard, they would contact the number on his business card, the one Connie and Natalie had been given when she'd hired him as a private investigator to find Bryce. Connie fingered the card in her hand. What had happened to Larry to cause his injuries? He was the favorite guard in Los Lagos, so shouldn't he have more support than just from her and Jaeda?

She told Melanie about seeing Larry at Spine Scottsdale, but she hadn't really gotten much information from him. Jaeda was so well trained to be a discreet banker, and he was busy hovering over Connie during her physical therapy that he didn't pry much. Men! Why couldn't they be nosey like women?

The next morning she rang the number on his business card. His voice rang clear and professional. Connie took the lead. "Need to meet with you, Larry. You need to share so we can help."

Chapter Twenty-eight
Connie and Melanie
Meeting with Larry

They met at the Starbucks in Safeway. Fry's Market was closer, but the visiting area was cozier in Safeway. Besides, the parking lot had tented areas of shade. With temperatures in Arizona hovering near a hundred plus, the car would stay cooler. Soon it would be July with temps in three digits all the time.

Larry insisted on paying for their Frappuccino's. He set them on a round Formica table where the women were settled into a corner booth. "Explain, please," Connie said. "I know you've shared a lot with Melanie, but Jaeda and I really care."

He frowned and pursed his lips so the neat moustache above them spread a little more across his mouth. After he twirled his cup a few times, he cleared his throat and spoke hesitantly. "Not a pretty picture." He seemed to hesitate again. "You ladies know what my cycle is like? How different it is, and how small?"

"Sort of," Connie said. "I think it's the same kind Jaeda has. A Yamaha R1, right?"

"Vivian Lord has one, too. I'm pretty sure," Melanie added.

"Really?" Larry's eyebrows raised high in question. "Knew that about Jaeda, but not about Mrs. Lord. She wasn't home when I stayed at their house with Bill."

"No," Connie said. "She was here, helping me."

Connie was obviously getting impatient. The babies must be competing in gymnastics, and when he looked over at her, he was sure he saw her belly moving all around, almost gyrating. "Can't stay too long, Larry, so please tell us what happened. Exactly," she added. She inched back from the table against the Vinyl seat. Maybe to give her gyrating belly more room.

He decided to spill it all out. "It started when I left Nat's house in Newport Beach, in Eastbluff, sometime in the evening after dusk. I try not to ride long distances in dark in places I'm not familiar with because the Yamaha is small. I wanted to spend as much time as possible with her. We had had a great weekend; I even got dragged to church, and it wasn't bad." He grinned and twisted the coffee cup again. He took a sip. Perhaps it would calm his gravelly throat.

"I was going up, maybe climbing is a better word, San Juaquin Hills Road. It's a steep street."

The women nodded. They knew it well.

"I was a bit confused about how to get to the

121

freeway, so probably shouldn't have taken that route. Anyway, I did. Then, I heard a rumble, a loud one." He finally took a drawn-out sip through the long straw and bent his head. "I knew it was cycles, so being on one, I felt comfortable, even okay. Until . . ."

Connie glanced at Melanie's face. Her eyes were locked on Larry's. What was that tingling feeling in the air? She shook her head, to clear it? She clasped her hands tightly above her belly until her knuckles were white. Larry must have noticed because he jumped back into the story.

"I don't think they were a gang of Hell's Angels, but I think they were rowdy kids showing off." He looked puzzled, then continued. "Are kids allowed to have motorcycles, Harleys?"

Both women nodded, but Connie spoke. "Yep. Unfortunately, in Newport some parents give the kids motorcycles as birthday and grad gifts. Too much opulence," she sneered. She released her hands and cupped them below her tummy. "Go on."

"There were three of them, maybe more. It was dark, and everything happened so fast. They surrounded me, forced me off the road. I had no choice. I'm not ashamed to say I was scared. Didn't know what they had in mind. I could hear their chants, and their laughter. I think they were on something, drugs or booze. Or, maybe brought up to be bigoted."

Connie gasped. "Go on, please. What did they say?"

Larry's face paled. "Have you ever heard the vilest expression used to call an African American?

Just one simple word."

"Oh, Larry." Connie nodded. She knew the word. She felt miserable. She reached for his hand across the small table. She told Larry about the incident at the Newport Pavilion when she and Jaeda had their first date, when that horrible girl Vicki from her high school class resisted touching his hand, as if his color might rub off on her. She put a hand to her throat as if she was swallowing back bile.

She squeezed Larry's fingers hard. "Stupid people can be so cruel."

"I know you understand, Connie." Larry rubbed his forehead with a Starbucks napkin and looked at it. Waving it over the table, he grinned. "See, no color came off." They all laughed at his self-deprecating joke. It broke the tension.

"I had no choice but to veer off the side of the road. My cycle slammed into a tree and crumbled. Total disaster. I stumbled to the road, glad the evil teens were gone – laughing all the way up the road. Fortunately, I was alive. Or, as you would say, I was blessed." This time he grinned.

"None of the kids stopped to see how I was. I guess that was good in a way. I felt like I'd been beaten up, but it was the crash into the tree when I flew off the cycle that gave me all my injuries."

"Who stopped? Did someone try to help you?" Connie was now on the edge of her seat. Her coffee was probably lukewarm, but she didn't care. She leaned forward to hear the rest of Larry's story.

"A kind man, a gentleman. Somehow, I blurted out Nat's name, and he said he knew her. I think I have his card." He dug in his pocket and pulled out

Logan Lovejoy's real estate business card.

"Oh, Larry, I don't believe in coincidences. God sent Mr. Lovejoy to rescue you," Connie declared. She felt her eyes misting. Melanie spoke almost in tandem with Connie.

"Larry, Logan is the father of Braydon who married our Candy Cane sister, Noelle; and, the father of Rob who married Cindy, another Candy Cane sister." She looked at him quizzically. "You do know about the Candy Canes, don't you?"

The skin around his eyes wrinkled; he nodded and chuckled. "Yep, Nat gave me the lowdown. In depth," he added with a grin. "You girls are a team."

Chapter Twenty-nine
Melanie
Confession

Connie sat stunned in the red recliner. Jaeda and Melanie hunkered on the sofa. Nobody said a word. Three pairs of eyes stared into space. Melanie spoke in a muffled whisper. "Now you know. Horrible, huh?"

Connie fiddled with the hem of her oversized top; Jaeda didn't move, just stared ahead. Finally, he looked at his beloved. "This could have happened to me, to us, Con."

She nodded with tears streaming down her pale cheeks. Melanie spoke in a shaky voice. "It could have been worse. They could have beaten him. Or, he could have been killed." She looked at her two friends and asked the question hovering in her mind. "Would it have been worse in Scottsdale?"

Both of them, Jaeda and Connie, shook their

heads. "No," Jaeda spoke first. "We have a lot of mixed racial couples here. Many in our church. Even one of our white, female pastors is married to a black man. We feel comfortable here." Shaking his head, he added, "But we really had no problems in Newport, either."

Suddenly, Melanie perked up, and standing up, made an announcement. "I love him!"

Chapter Thirty
Larry
Decision

Larry could hardly believe the girl with the soft brown, curly hair loved him. She had taken him to Hillsong Church in Scottsdale several times in the last few weeks. It brought back memories of going to church with his Da. Those hadn't been often, more sporadic after his mom left. The passion was the same – raising hands in praise during the songs, yelling out "Amen" during the message. He wondered why they were called messages now and not sermons. A moot point he decided. But, the messages so often based on God's forgiveness and Jesus' sacrifice haunted him.

He had traveled to Newport again, this time to visit Melanie. Again, he stayed at Bill and Vivian Lord's house. He saw and began to understand the interaction among all the people there. They were friends based on faith. He had attended church with Melanie both in Scottsdale and when he visited Newport Beach. Something tugged at his heart. Was it Melanie, or God? Would God know his secret? Should he tell Melanie?

Finally, one Sunday back in Scottsdale at Hillsong Church, sitting close to Melanie, the Church News came on the screen. It was a video explaining all that was happening and going to happen in the church. The one that held his attention was the one about baptisms next Sunday. Could he do it? Was he ready? He needed to be sure. In his heart and in his mind, also his soul. He turned to Melanie, and to Jaeda and Connie sitting next to her. "Please pray for me," is all he said.

~

Larry hadn't expected this to be such a party. Connie, Jaeda and Melanie stood next to the baptismal pool all grinning and cheering with iPhones clicking as his head was submerged by Pastor Tom. They dried him off with a fluffy towel and led him dripping to Jaeda's car. He heard cheering and loud "Praise God" from behind him for other baptisms. He was cold from the water, but warm in his heart. Suddenly, he felt like laughing. What a glorious feeling, so freeing. No matter his past, he was God's child now.

Chapter Thirty-one
Connie
Questions

Connie could hardly believe she was designing wedding attire again. It had only been a year since she'd designed the elegant lace bridal gown and the crazy, multi-colored attendants' dresses for Emily who married Claire's son, Nick, in Nat's Gym. A few days ago she'd rushed the new blue pastel fabric and designs to Sandy who cut and sewed them during a few long nights making double overtime. What a gift that woman is.

Melanie was back in Scottsdale to visit her wedding gown designer. "I'm not a virgin, Connie. You know that. You know I lost a baby a long time ago. It was heartbreaking. He was a boy. So," she continued after dabbing at her eyes, "I don't want to be married in white, at least not pure white." She looked at Connie hoping her friend would understand.

Connie pulled Mel close in her arms as best she could over her enormous baby bump that was way more than a bump now. "Of course, I understand completely, and I'm grateful you reminded me. I respect that about you, Mel." Connie grabbed a stack from a pile of wedding magazines on the little table in her work room. The girls had been chatting about bridesmaids' dresses when Melanie made her blue announcement. Leafing through the magazines, both were happy to see that white was not as popular or traditional as it had been. Many colors, mostly pastel ones with soft whitish tints, jumped out at them for bridal gowns. They found an idea from one that was blue with white tulle overlay. Connie thought it was almost ethereal. Mel was so thrilled with the idea she whispered, "My God color." Connie looked at her quizzically. Melanie shrugged and said, "Some things can't be explained." Connie smiled.

Connie had loved designing all the gowns for the Candy Cane brides, and she knew they all loved what she had produced. Emily's, although she was not a designated Candy Cane, had been the most challenging. It was almost entirely lace, and figuring out how to attach the delicate sleeves and bodice, and even the wrists, without using any under fabric became an experiment. Finally, she decided on invisible thread. The gown was so gorgeous she started featuring it on her website and in brochures. She never copied it, but the idea had brought a lot of attention to Winning Designs, and a lot of money.

She shifted on her stool and closed her eyes. She always did that when designing for a real person, and she visualized Melanie in a blueish bridal gown. Tiny narrow ribbons and minute blue sequins danced before her eyes. Flowing white silk would still be the underlay, but blue, very pastel, would be sprinkled liberally over it, shimmering to catch the light. Melanie had decided on an illusion neckline in front and a heart-shaped opening in the back, the entire bodice in lace. Connie was excited. She had never attempted to design such a complicated gown, other than Emily's, but she could do it. The lace part was still a challenge. Not so much for the design part, but for the delicate and extensive cutting, pining and sewing. She knew Sandy could do it, and would do it with perfection. Normally, she would have helped Sandy, worked alongside of her. Two little beings in her tummy prevented her from bending over the cutting table. Besides, there was no way she could get close to a sewing machine.

She set to work and sent the design to Sandy. Fortunately, Connie had a stash of fabrics and all the ingredients. Jaeda would drive them over later. The wedding was less than a week away, but Sandy seemed to be a miracle worker when it came to producing almost instant couture.

~

She was tired. Not even sure why she was still sitting at her designing table since Melanie's wedding designs were in production and close to ready. Maybe habit, routine, a break from designing layettes. She loved coming up with unique ideas for newborn clothes and matching parent clothes, but her brain was on halt. Putting her pen and pencils back in the container on the corner of her tilted drawing table, she started to slide off the high stool, this time more carefully. Her hands grasped under her stomach to steady it. What was that stabbing pain? It was in her back. Strange.

Not Braxton Hicks. Those usually occurred in the tummy she'd been told. Oh, well, she would check on the crockpot. This time it was a chicken dish. Jaeda loved chicken. The wedding was in two days. Tonight she would rest.

Chapter Thirty-two
The Wedding

A small number, maybe fifty, were gathered closely near the front in the large worship auditorium of Hillsong Church in Scottsdale. It wasn't a big crowd, but the most important crowd. Friends.

Natalie thought Melanie shined. Most of her brown hair was swept up in a flowing chignon clasped with silver surrounded in blue stones. The rest of her locks fell softly on her shoulders like a curly cascade. She was holding tightly to the gift Nat had given her – a small pink Bible wrapped in flowers and ribbons. Melanie glowed with peace marrying the man she loved. Her mother, Helen, was beside her, the beaming Matron of Honor. Natalie was glad she and Mel had finally reconnected again. She herself beamed as the Maid of Honor. After all, she had introduced Melanie and Larry. Noelle, Connie, Candy, Doreen, and Cindy, who was fortunately still in the states, glowed in shimmering pastel blue gowns. What a blessing that they'd all traveled to Scottsdale for Mel and Larry. She saw Jaeda as Best Man fiddling with a hand in his pocket. The ring? She'd felt so privileged when Larry showed it to her. She was also shocked by its shape and color. It was a spectacular heart-shaped diamond sparkling with the palest blue hue in a platinum band set with minute sapphires.

Since they hadn't had a long engagement, actually none at all, he decided to give Melanie a combo ring, one signifying their love for each other; one in her God color. He told Natalie he hadn't known there was such a thing as a blue diamond, but he'd been blown away to find it, on an internet site of all places. He had ordered it and received it within two days by special courier, then took it to a local renowned jeweler to make sure it was the real deal. He was amazed again when the noted jeweler told him the value. He truly had gotten a real deal. Nat remembered his hands shook when he showed it to her, and she understood why. Dabbing an eye with a tissue, she gave Larry a kiss on his blushing cheek. She had been honored to read the inscription. "Your love for me, and your love for the Lord, will bless us both forever."

Nat suppressed the memory to dwell on later and checked inside her bouquet. Yes, Mel's wide platinum band to Larry was still there. The single minute diamond matched the ones in his ears. She had taken the liberty of reading the inscription, and her heart swelled. "Larry and Mel ~ Loving God and each other for Eternity."

She wished she could have taken a photo of the bridal party. Hopefully, the photographer they'd hired would. This was a memory she wanted to hold in her heart forever. Her best friend marrying her own former, almost lover. She was happy beyond imagination for Larry and Melanie. Still, she wondered about Mel's reaction to the tattoos on their cruise honeymoon. They had all seen them when he got baptized, but he did have a tee shirt on, and swim trunks.

She knew they had a stateroom with a balcony and the cruise line's equivalent of a king bed. How she would love to be a fly on the wall just to see Mel's reaction to handsome Larry's full body of tattoos. She put her blue painted fingertips to her lips. She mustn't, mustn't, chuckle. She felt positive in her heart that Mel was so in love with Larry after their short courtship she would love all the body inkings. Except, maybe, the flaming cross one. Now that he had been baptized, maybe he would try to have it removed. Or, altered. Maybe not.

For the first time in a Candy Cane wedding, Braydon and Love In Joy Floral did not provide or design the flowers. Marg at North Scottsdale Floral produced beautiful nosegay bouquets wrapped in lace for the women and an elegant, flowing one with a lot of blue flowers trailing in it for Melanie. Braydon stood next after Jaeda with Bill, Sr. and Bill, Jr. and Candy's husband, Devin, who was also a groomsman. Was there a sixth man to balance out the number of bridesmaids? Aw, Candy's brother, Billy Ashford, took up the rear, the last of the groomsmen.

Her eyes got huge when she saw another man slip into the front row. What was Bryce doing here? Why was his hair cut? No ponytail?

Just before the song to lead the bridesmaids down the aisle, she heard a commotion. She looked around to see all six of the women. Noelle just a few months pregnant looked radiant, Cindy glowed with the Lord's light, Candy's face still shined from her recent remarriage to Devin. Doreen looked stately and elegant as always, and Connie who had supported Mel's decision would waddle down the aisle last. Connie had tried to bow out of the ceremony; she hadn't wanted to detract from it or the bride because of her enormous belly, but Mel insisted. Melanie even quipped about wanting her bridal "couture designer" in the wedding party.

Melanie's mother, Helen Carson, first to step in place as Matron of Honor turned to smile at the others. Suddenly, her expression froze, and putting a hand to her satiny pink lips, she shrieked.

The music stopped.

Chapter Thirty-three
Connie and Jaeda
Surprise!

Connie felt horrible. Even though she still had erratic threads of pain in her lower back, she reminded herself the twins weren't due for another few weeks. She hadn't told Jaeda about the pains because they hadn't concerned her much. Now, feeling streams of moisture running down her legs, she wished she had.

The twins decided to enter this world on the most inappropriate day. She had no control over that, but she succumbed to the pains. What else could she do?

Jaeda held her hand and led her through the birthing exercises. She was wheeled into an operating room, not the normal hospital birthing room she had hoped for. Dr. Francois was there, and seventeen other doctors. She explained one would hold the girl back by pushing on Connie's tummy, so she could be born second. That way the two babies could be born individually and the girl wouldn't flip or push on her brother. The other doctors were there "just in case." She tried to not think about that phrase.

Little Lawrence Jaeda was born first at 6:15. Melanie Natalie was born three minutes later waving a tiny hand. Dr. Francois joked about little Mel coming out like a beauty queen with the perfect wave. Connie succumbed to tears. Happy ones, exhausted ones. She praised God the twins hadn't needed to be taken by C-section. She wanted a natural birth, and Dr. Francois had given her that. The amazing babies were each over six pounds, so unusual for twins, especially first born. No wonder she had been so huge and encumbered. She remembered several of the doctors gasping when little Lawrence was born. She heard whispers. "White?" and "What?" One even said "One in five hundred. A miracle?"

She learned later that night while cuddling two babies in her arms that Melanie had stopped the wedding for their births. She wanted to have it in Honor Health Hospital so Connie and Jaeda could attend. Surely, she couldn't be serious. She also learned Jaeda had a primo bank client (does fifty plus accounts tally for that?) who was on the board of the hospital. That's why he left her for twenty minutes after cuddling his newborn son. Her husband was a special guy.

Connie and Jaeda, both holding babies, settled into a makeshift pew in the front row of the Honor Health Hospital event area now converted to a wedding venue. Connie almost laughed out loud seeing a wedding banner had been stretched and anchored across the sign for the Diagnostic Center. Must have been the nurses or the hospital staff. Neither baby squirmed, but she held Mel Nat to her breast under a thin blanket. Little Larry snored lightly in Jaeda's arms making Connie giggle. Just like his father.

The area was perfect for a wedding. A little more public than having it in a church, but there was a grand piano just behind a huge round planter filled with a massive Ficus tree. Candles in glass globes and potted blooms rested all along on the circular wall of the planter. The heady scent of flowers was abundant. Some had been brought from the auditorium at Hillsong Church, from the originally planned wedding. She learned later, the nurses and support staff at the hospital not only donated many of them, but arranged them. They were beautiful. Connie's heart sang for Mel and Larry.

A volunteer, a young man on the hospital staff, sat on the piano bench. The Hillsong praise band, led by Hillsong's own Dr. George on his electronic keyboard, strummed on their guitars. It was a muted praise song Connie didn't recognize. Something about praising God and the Holy Spirit filling them.

Helen, Noelle, Cindy, Doreen, Natalie and Candy floated down the short makeshift aisle formed by white folding chairs on two sides. How beautiful they looked in their pastel blue gowns. All were the same filmy fabric, but each woman's was slightly different in length and bodice. Noelle's was high-cut and skimmed around her calves. Natalie's was a simple sheath. Candy's was long touching her shoes. Cindy's was demure, with cap sleeves and the skirt resting on her knees. Helen's was topped by a shawl that shimmered in the candlelight. Doreen's was slim, long and split slightly on the side of her good leg. Connie had designed each gown for each lovely woman. All their shoes were silver.

Connie stood up with the rest when the wedding march played on the piano signifying Melanie's turn as the bride to float down the aisle. Connie still had little Mel Nat clutched to her breast, but the blanket was over her shoulder. Suddenly, the baby burst into a yell. So loud for a newborn, but Mel Nat was a born actress according to Dr. Francois. Connie tried to comfort her, but she wouldn't stop. She tried to scoot past Jaeda to leave the wedding when Melanie in her luminous gown stopped in the aisle just before reaching the alter. She practically seized the baby from Connie's arms, cuddling her close. Connie released her precious bundle to the arms of her new aunt. "My namesake," Melanie whispered so loud Connie was sure all heard her. The baby stopped crying.

Melanie carried the baby to the alter still snuggled into her neck. She held her all during the ceremony. With dramatically raised brows, Jaeda lifted baby Larry into Connie's now empty arms before he rose to stand next to the groom. Finally, the vows and rings had been exchanged and the pastor, who looked so confused Connie was sure he might pass out, pronounced them husband and wife. Melanie and Larry turned to race up the aisle hand in hand trying to kiss over the now quiet infant in her arms.

Larry was laughing, and Melanie paused by the front row where Connie sat. She surrendered her baby bundle and gently shifted the now sleeping child into Connie's arms with a blown kiss and a "Thank you."

Epilogue

Natalie sat at her desk in her gym, her silver clad feet propped up on it. She had flown back to Newport on the red eye still wearing her Maid of Honor gown and causing a lot of astonished stares. Even the normally composed flight attendants raised eyebrows. She had ignored them all. She did not want to impose again at Jaeda and Connie's. Although Connie would be staying at Honor Health Hospital for at least another day, protocol to be sure the twins and she were healthy and could go home. Still, she needed to get home herself to sort things out.

Not sure why she was here at the gym instead of her home. Habit? She hoped that crazy, cute dog Lola was okay. Why had she agreed to babysit her? Fortunately, Pet Smart had an opening, and when she took Lola there, the funny dog was very excited. *Guess she, like most of us, wants companionship.*

Natalie knew she did. She would pick Lola up in the morning, after coffee.

She rubbed her eyes with the heels of her hands and smeared blue mascara over her cheeks. What had happened at Mel's wedding? She was astonished, and grateful, that Melanie had stopped the wedding until the next day, until the twins were born, and decided to hold it in a smaller venue. It had been a lovely wedding, except for the unusual bit when Mel held the baby in her arms during the ceremony. Nat couldn't get her mind around that. Holding a newborn, not even one's own, in the bride's arms during a marriage? She was excited for Melanie and Larry, but had Melanie been in her senses? It was like a bottle thrown into the ocean washing up on the shore, then breaking to reveal the secret letter stuffed in it so long ago.

What about two different colored babies? Little Mel Nat was a dark-skinned girl with a crop of tight black curls. She was beautiful, and even Natalie could imagine her becoming an actress someday and a diva. The yell she let out just before the ceremony sounded like an announcement from an artiste. Someday she would surely be on stage. Her brother, Lawrence Jaeda, the calm one, slept contentedly, his pale skin challenging his parentage. What had happened? A God thing? DNA? An anomaly? Two different colored babies from the same two people. Not for her to figure out.

The reception had been in the hospital's flagstone patio across from the cafeteria. It had been fantastic. Honor Health Hospital had graciously offered to cater. Its kitchen did make yummy Caesar salad, her favorite. The Starbucks Frappuccino bar was a wonderful touch. The Hillsong praise band broke loose with dance music. Nat had found herself swinging and twirling with Bryce of all people. She even danced with Billy Carson who had nuzzled her ear. Unfortunately, he hadn't offered to drive her back to Newport Beach in a Maserati. She heard herself giggling. Too late, Larry, and Bryce, and Billy. She was ruminating too much. She had no Larry, surely no Bryce, and probably no Billy. Was her mystery man out there somewhere?

It had all been so strange. She remembered touching up her makeup right before the ceremony in the elaborate hospital restroom while Connie nursed the babies in the special area for nursing mothers. She remembered walking down the white aisle made of folded bedsheets by the nursing staff and bordered by white folding chairs on either side. Mostly, she recalled making sure the ring for Larry was secure in her bouquet. The rest was a blur, except for a baby crying right before the ceremony.

She kicked off her shoes. Six a.m. The reception had lasted and lasted. Blue was definitely the theme, even the punch was blue. So many people showing so much love.

She needed to get home.

She turned the key in the ignition of her little convertible, an exorbitant present to herself. She imagined the cool Pacific breeze freeing her hair from the chignon, the song of the wind whispering in her ears and its breath blowing the mascara streaks off her cheeks. Natalie was ready for another chapter in her life. Until her cell phone rang. She let it go to voicemail because she was driving. Why was Melanie calling her on her honeymoon? When she drove into her drive, she parked to listen to the message and collapsed against the steering wheel in a puddle of tears.

Nat, I need you. We were in line to board the ship when two FBI agents grabbed Larry by the arms and arrested him for identity theft. I don't know what to do. My husband is gone. Please help.

Nat pulled herself up, wiped her eyes with the hem of her gown and blew her nose in a crumpled tissue. She kept going over in her mind about Larry. There were a few times, moments really, when he had seemed evasive. Like he had been trying to hide something. But, the moments were fleeting. So much that Natalie, and obviously Melanie, had shoved them out of their thoughts. Everyone had some secrets, so no big deal. And she'd heard Jaeda said when meeting Larry at Spine Scottsdale, "not our beeswax."

Wiping her face with the soggy tissue, she finally told Melanie to take a Uber and come back to Nat's. She would pay for it and wait up for her. Tomorrow they would contact a lawyer for Larry and find out more. Tonight they both needed sleep. Tomorrow, as Annie said in the famous play, "tomorrow is another day." She immediately thought of the the Days and the Lovejoys, especially since Logan Lovejoy had witnessed Larry's horrible accident and taken over by calling 911 and the police and the insurance company. He was a prominent realtor. Maybe he would have a suggestion for a lawyer to help Larry. He would be the first one to call.

She remembered a quote on a Facebook page that spoke to her about horrible situations. She'd googled the man's name. He was a Bible teacher and pastor. She would cling to these words. "A faith that hasn't been tested can't be trusted." - Adrian Rogers

"How Lord, why?" Nat whispered hoping for a whisper from God. Hearing none, she went indoors and turned on all the lights, and waited for Melanie.

The End

Enjoy the first chapter of book 7, Melanie's Ghosts

Prologue

"This is wrong. No sense. Makes no sense."

Melanie embraced his big, strong brown hand between her small white ones. Larry didn't move. He was dead.

~

Melanie sat across the table from attorney Randi. Her fingers were paste white and knuckles blue. Is that what death does? She examined her glittering fingernails; the fancy ones Kay had gifted her with for her marriage to Larry and now insisted she needed again as a boost for the burial. But, their luster was useless. Her life was, too. Her future held no meaning. She was a widow, not a newlywed.

Natalie, her best friend, shifted in her chair. "What is the next step, Randi? Melanie needs somewhere to go in her heart and in her head. She needs to find understanding and peace. What do you suggest?" She looked over at Mel and squeezed her hand, the hand that rested on her special blue skirt, the one she clung to and claimed as her God skirt, the one she wore when she met Larry. What would happen to the skirt now? Would it be folded away in a memory trunk, or maybe destroyed?

Randi, professional attorney as she was, blinked rapidly. Moisture coated her lashes. "I have been trying to decide how to tell you. Not easy."

"Just tell, please. I need to know what to do." Melanie squeezed Natalie's hand tighter.

Randi sighed and pushed a paper toward the two women.

"A list? You are giving me a list?"

"No, I am giving you a suggestion. Hopefully a healing option." She lowered her chin. "Sorry. But I believe this is the one thing that will give you comfort and clarity."

Melanie picked up the typewritten paper, the paper with the single suggestion, and held it in trembling hands. Natalie leaned closer to look. "Oh!" The expletive blew out of her mouth like a gust of dry wind.

Chapter One
Melanie

Newport Beach is a strangely diverse community. Or, should I say town? It claims to be a city, but when you daily run into neighbors in the market or at church or taking a jog, it's really a town.

What is strange about its diversity isn't that it's not all lily white. Not completely. There is the Yu family down the block and Dr. Hawthorne the black doctor who is part of the primary care physician group in Fashion Island. No, what's strange about its diversity isn't ethnicity or color or age. It's the groupings. The family homes, the planned communities as they used to be called; the lavish apartment homes, too pricey for short-term dwellers; the cute condo communities, the ones the empty-nesters downsize to; the raggly, straggly beach bungalows bordering the edge of the bay – summer homes for the financially secure, some who actually live in lavish homes on the hill but want to play on the beach.

I grew up in one of the condos in Eastbluff. Well, mostly. When my mom's first marriage dissolved, the one after my dad died and she was lonely, we moved from our tract house, the one in the planned community that she and dad had never remodeled. They couldn't afford to. Still, it sold for five times the price they'd paid for it in the seventies. That's how much Newport was sought after for a small plot of land and an old, simple three small bedroom house to be torn down and rebuilt. Crazy.

When Mom and I moved to our cozy condo in The Bluffs I didn't mind. In fact, I loved it. I still attended Vista del Mar High School and could even walk there. I was a slightly above average student with no sights set on a Big Five University. Never athletic, although sports were revered at VDM, I envied the slim, bustless girls who garnered so much attention winning state and regional swim championships. The Candy Canes they were called. For some reason they were allowed to form a team within a team and were also allowed to choose their own swimsuits. Maybe Speedo designed those special red and white striped suits just for them. Maybe because everyone, especially Coach Beckworth, knew they were deemed to be champions. A much-needed accolade for a beach community school way too focused on football.

I will never know if it was fate, God's plan or my stupidity that caused the accident. I had been partying, driving my beloved new red pick-up on Coast Highway. Distracted, and drunk, I ran a red light. That night I met forgiveness. Five girls and a young man surrounded me in a waiting area of Hoag Hospital while Doreen's leg was being operated on, maybe even amputated. The strangest part was those girls and that man, Braydon Lovejoy, prayed for me almost as much as they prayed for Doreen whose life I had almost taken, and certainly damaged.

That's when I knew, that's when I got it.

Faith. Forgiveness. Friendship.

Read the rest here

Meet Bonnie

I love connecting with my readers, so I hope you will write to me at bengstrom@hotmail.com and especially tell me what you want to see happen to Larry and Melanie, and Natalie. Your ideas inspire me. I feed on them.

My husband Dave and I were blessed to raise our three children in Newport Beach, California. When our first grandchild, Miss Mookie, was born twelve years ago in Arizona we moved to Scottsdale to be near to her. Now, she has three siblings, a younger sister, and two of whom are twins, a boy and a girl. We don't miss Newport at all, except for our wonderful friends and neighbors, and Bible study fellowships. Now, we spend many afternoons picking kids up after school and taking them to gymnastics, doctor appointments and chess tournaments. It's a different life we thrive on.

We both thought we would retire. Didn't happen. I am especially blessed to be multi-published by Forget Me Not Romances, a dream come true. Dave quips he is the oldest new hire in the U.S. by accepting the position as a Core Counseling Faculty member at the University of Phoenix, for which he also teaches many online classes. He is on the staff at Honor Health Hospital in Scottsdale where he teaches pre-op and post-op classes for bariatric surgery. Honor Health is recognized in several of my books. Not a surprise!

Our grandparenting and our situations keep us busy.

To meet all of our grandchildren read *Cindy's Perfect Dance*. They all play a part in Cindy and Rob's wedding on the beach in Costa Rica. Or, visit my website at www.bonnieengstrom.com to see Dave and me with the crew.

Please email me at bengstrom@hotmail.com. Be sure to put BOOK in the subject line so you don't get lost in my junk mail file.

Thank you for reading my books. Writing them for you is a privilege and a blessing.

Author Note

This book is the sixth in the Candy Cane Girls Series.

If you are new to this series it may be a bit confusing, especially with so many characters, so many women and so many men, and two dogs. I've tried to highlight each of them to help you understand them and become friends with them. As Melanie says in the beginning, this is a story about all of them as friends. Their lives do intertwine in countless ways. I hope you enjoy each separate mini-story and take Melanie's advice to read from the first Candy Cane story about Noelle and her Christmas wedding. Every woman has her own special story, and you can be part of each. Blessings, Bonnie

Don't miss the other books in the series: